THE DISCIPLE

BETTER

TO

DO

EVIL

THAN

TO

BE

EVIL

BILL HULL

Book & jacket design by KR15 Creative Services [KR15.com]
Set in Adobe Garamond & Gotham

ISBN (paperback) 978-0-9910041-2-6
ISBN (Kindle edition) 978-0-9910041-3-3

First edition: December 2013
Printed in the USA

CONTENTS

PROLOGUE

Michael Hart took his bloody hand and rubbed the fog off the inside of his windshield. It was 2:38 AM and his heart was pounding as he strained to see if Clarke had left the house yet.

He was already having second thoughts on why he had let Tommy Boy help him. Killing is a precise business if you want to get away with it. But since Clarke was the reason he was in this mess, it made some sense for him to be the cleaner.

Years earlier in Bosnia, Tom Clarke had been a cleaner. After an assassination, someone had to make sure all evidence was gone: no sign of entry, no records of any kind, all phones, computers, every clue destroyed. But Tommy was rusty, to say the least, and hadn't been sober much since 1997. He was the kind of guy who never missed an opportunity to miss an opportunity.

Here Clarke came, bounding over a hedge, sliding to the car, and slapping into the seat with his full weight. "Got everything?"

"Yeah, think so." Tommy was nervous as he spoke, his voice as tense as the moment. Two dead men with their throats slit, one in the hallway, the other on the back steps, both killed by the Reverend Michael Hart. It wasn't a story he could tell in his Sunday sermon. Michael loved the feel of the Porsche 911 as it shot out of the motionless neighborhood, over eighty K—too bad he couldn't keep it. The car dealer on 96th Street would miss it in a few hours, but he would never find it. Michael knew about these things. Most of it he never talked about; only his troubled friend Tom Clarke understood.

— 1 —
INDY

Michael Hart had met his wife, Jennifer, at an Inter-Varsity International Missions Conference in Chicago. He was a third-year divinity student at Trinity in Deerfield, and she was a senior at Wheaton College. It was one of those magical moments when they were assigned to the same discussion group. Jen was a 5–7 blond with a body that, Michael liked to say, "would make a bishop kick his foot through stained glass."

She was vivacious and opinionated, with that "let's get out of here and have some fun" look in her eye. They were both stars, they liked the limelight, and they liked each other a lot. Their first kiss was passionate, and they had no stop button; only their circumstances and convictions held them back.

Michael was 5–11, 180, athletic, and confident. His sandy hair and blue eyes reminded girls of Robert Redford. He was a Hoosier from the hamlet called Broad Ripple on the north side of Indianapolis. Jen was from old money, but the small-town old money of Elkhart, Indiana. He was raised a Catholic at Immaculate Heart of Mary on 56th and Central; she was raised at St. John's Episcopal. There weren't too many Episcopalians in Elkhart, but they had money, and they were in charge. They were the kind of exclusive society that shopped on the Miracle Mile of Michigan Avenue, held sponsored invitation-only debutante balls, and sent their daughters to Wheaton.

Jen was a Vanderwal. She was raised to expect life to come with certain accoutrements, including certain ones that her family would insist on seeing in a husband. Michael, Catholic and hopelessly working class, came without aristocratic portfolio and with a massive student loan. And to add injury, now he was neither Catholic nor Episcopalian but a theological mongrel. Still, all the differences didn't seem to matter; they had explosive chemistry. Wheaton and Trinity had made them both zealous believers, what some would call disciples. It was a world missions conference that brought them together, and together they would stay.

Jen slapped Michael on the butt. "Get out of bed, dude." Michael slept in the nude, an old and pajamas-saving tradition. He tried to get Jen to do the same, but to no avail.

"Come on, get in the shower. The kids are almost ready." Jen had that mischievous look in her eye as she ripped off her nightgown and ran for the shower. Fourteen years married and Michael was still thrilled to see the "bishop's body" luscious before him. He bounced out of bed and ran toward the bathroom in one motion, no stop button anywhere, none needed.

✻ ✻ ✻

"You're late, Dad. You are never late. I'm going to be tardy."

Eight-year-old Janie rarely withheld her opinion. "I know, Janie; we'll make it. Even if we don't, I'll take the blame."

Corey, earbuds in, was listening to Radiohead again, something Michael detested since all he could remember from their catalogue was *"Creep"*: *"I'm a creep, I'm a weirdo, what am I doing here…I want a perfect body, I want a perfect soul,"* and then a few F-bombs. He wanted to protect his son from that kind of crap. None of that alienated loser "oh woe is me, give me a drug, a gun, a like-minded girl so

I can screw up my life" stuff for his boy. But of course Michael believed Corey was listening to some benign Christian singer talk to God like He was her boyfriend.

Michael was feeling great about the extra ten minutes he'd had with Jen as he screeched into a handicapped parking spot. No problem; he was the pastor and the school met in his church. Life was good. Heads turned as the Hart clan spilled out of the car and Corey and Janie sprinted for class.

Michael smiled at his "fans" and swung his backpack over his right shoulder. He had the walk of a man with an entourage; he didn't just show up for work but made personal appearances. He was a religious star, people loved him, he had a factory-installed smile, and his face looked positive and upbeat even when it was at rest. He high-fived some of the kids as he made his way through the hallway to his office.

His rise to local fame had been supersonic. He and Jen had returned to his home town of Indianapolis after they graduated, determined to start a church they both would like to attend. Newly married, Michael spurned an offer to join Jen's father in banking. G. Ralph Vanderwal was CEO of Northern Indiana Bank and Trust, a string of very successful small-town banks stretching from Clearlake in the east to Chesterton in the west. It would guarantee Michael and Jen a life of power and small-town prestige, but they didn't even have to think about it; the answer was no.

They had a great name for the church: The Challenge. That was how they saw it. Life in Christ was about the challenge to follow Him and to convince the rest of the world to do the same. The Challenge began in September of 2002 with a group of fourteen—fifteen if you counted Corey, still in Jen's womb.

It took Michael ten minutes to run the gauntlet to his office. The school principal stopped him for advice, but mostly parents and kids wanted his attention. The main building was 100,000 square feet, surrounded by smaller support buildings with beautiful courtyards, foundations, and sculpture gardens, the kind of ambiance that both he and Jen had wanted. A church that didn't look like a church, where people would love to stroll, talk, relax, and enjoy the beautiful creation of God and man. The school had nine hundred students in grades one through eight. The high school was in the planning stage and would open the next year with a freshman class.

In Las Vegas, the casinos had created mini-Paris in the desert. It was Michael's and Jen's dream to create the look of a classy Florentine villa in the flat fields of Central Indiana—Tuscany surrounded by cornstalks, the Uffizi bordered by I-465. Not only did the gospel need a renaissance, so did the look of Christians. Michael and Jen's vacations and art tours in Florence provided the vision for such things. Walking down a church hallway was like walking through a great museum because here and there hung Annunciation by Leonardo or The Deposition by Rosso Fiorentino. Michelangelo's David created a brief scandal when it appeared in the newest garden, but its beauty finally overwhelmed even its most ardent enemies. Michael had found it interesting what one could adjust to if it was beautiful—especially when all the art was donated by private money and drew many visitors to Sunday services.

Michael finally breezed into his personal assistant's office. Millie had been with him from the start. She and her late husband, Herschel, were part of the now-famous original fourteen that started The Challenge. It had changed; more than 10,000 parishioners now poured through the doors every weekend.

"Mayor Ballard is on hold. I told him you were here," Millie said with some exasperation. Seven years with Michael had taught her never to promise that he would be on time.

Michael threw his pack on the couch and grabbed the phone. "Mayor, how are you?" Michael made everyone feel special. Even Greg Ballard, the popular mayor of Indianapolis, came under Michael's spell.

"I'm fine, Michael. The Colts are looking good. Thought it would take Andrew Luck longer to adjust to the NFL." Both men loved the Indianapolis Colts, though the mayor was nervous about what another 2–14 season would do to the Indy brand and the downtown economy.

"I think Luck must have gone to class at Stanford," joked Michael. "He's smart and he's picking up the defensive schemes really fast. It was a good decision not to re-sign Peyton."

"Hey, Michael," Ballard interrupted, "got to have you speak again for the Mayor's Prayer Breakfast. I know you did it two years ago, but people want you back. Can you do it for me?"

Michael didn't need to think about this one. "Sure, Greg. For you, I'm there." Michael, a life long Hoosier, and a graduate of Butler University, loved his hometown. To help his mayor and his city, this was a no-brainer.

"Michael, I've got to go. I've got two tickets for Sunday night's game. I know you like down on the field rather than the box. These are sixth row. Do you want them?"

"You bet!" As they hung up, Michael was enthused. He could never make Sunday games because they were half over by the time he could get there. Three morning services not ending until 1:00 PM was not an NFL-friendly schedule. This game started at 8:00 PM; perfect.

He called Millie in for his daily briefing, not exactly a presidential CIA intelligence brief, but close. Millie was privy to all inner church intel, what some call gossip. Millie had a reputation in the coffee room and the cafeteria for having good ears and a discretionary filter. She would make sure Michael heard what he needed to but would discard the fluff. She was careful not to burden her beloved pastor with any unnecessary trash. Employees would speak loud enough around her or directly to her about their opinions and grievances, hoping that she would mention it to Michael. She was his mother protector, missing only the nun's habit.

"Frank Ewald wants another meeting with you about getting behind his effort to support the biblical definition of marriage." Millie smirked, because Frank Ewald believed that Michael should take a stand on many political matters.

"God has raised you up for such a time as this," Ewald would bellow. "Not to take advantage of your societal status is a sin."

Sanctimony dripped from each syllable. It was like listening to William Jennings Bryan at the height of his oratory.

"Isn't there someone else on staff to meet with him?" Michael was almost whining.

"No," snapped Millie. "Just shoot straight with him: you don't do politics!"

Shooting straight was not what Michael liked to do. He was very good at it when he had to be, but would rather avoid the fight. "Okay, put him in on Thursday afternoon. Next."

Millie ticked off the list: "Staff meeting at 1:30, bankers will be here to talk about funding for the new building at 3:00, Corey's flag football practice at 4:30, and Jen says dinner with the college staff at 6:30. And now you have chapel."

Michael leaned back. "Wow, what am I going to tell the students today? Haven't had time to think much about it." He sighed and grabbed his Bible.

He could hear the singing from the packed sanctuary, nearly a thousand students and staff gathered for the weekly chapel service. That would be the next thing, a bigger auditorium or satellite campuses spread through the city. Michael feared losing his grip on the congregation if he lost the power of personal presence.

He slipped into a seat near the front and felt his cell phone vibrate. Tom Clarke was calling; Michael had told him not to. Fear and anger welled up as he reached into his pocket and pressed the power button.

The kids erupted with applause, hoots, and whistles as their leader and founder walked onto the stage. They loved Michael because he was hip. He put the "hip" back into discipleship. That was the simple message: "We are to be disciples and make disciples. Jesus has called us, 'Follow me...'" That was The Challenge, and thousands of people on the north side of Indianapolis had decided to join Michael and Jen in that journey.

Michael's philosophy had been shaped by Dietrich Bonhoeffer and his literary masterpiece, *The Cost of Discipleship*. Bonhoeffer wrote that Jesus was the man for others. Michael preached that therefore, as Christ's followers, we exist for others, and the church exists for others. It was a bold vision, an exacting challenge. Michael's gift was that he made such a challenge so inviting that you wanted to join him on that same road. In a competitive world that seemed fit more for Howard Roark in Ayn Rand's *Fountainhead*, who said, "I don't exist for others," Michael made you want to do the opposite, like Jesus.

Michael gave a big fist pump, "How you doing, disciples?" he yelled. He called everyone "disciple." He didn't like the word *Christian*. It was hackneyed, it smacked of centuries of bad press, and followers of Jesus didn't call themselves that until the third century. *Disciple* was a more robust and descriptive word. It meant to follow, it meant to learn, it meant commitment. Michael wanted it to be the new norm of what it meant to follow Jesus.

— 2 —
NEW YORK

Alonzo Alvarez arose at 11:00 AM, early by his standards. Worrying about his younger brother had kept him up most of the night. He lit a cigarette and walked out onto his balcony overlooking Central Park. It was a long way from the Mexico City colonia where he learned the ways of the street as a boy. He made his first loan when he was nine to a twelve-year-old, a few pesos. When the kid didn't pay him back, Alvarez broke his toes with a hammer, and thus a star was born. When he was sixteen, under cover of darkness, he crawled across the US border at Tecate with enough money and connections to pay passage to New York City. He wanted to get deep into the country, to get lost in the crowd, to work his magic.

At five feet nine he was not big, but his muscular shoulders, heavily tattooed arms, and long dark hair made him a frightening sight to men and an attraction to certain women. He had dark eyes and a great smile and walked like he owned the space around him. Known as "AA" to his friends, he had learned English by watching television; with his sharp mind and fierce determination, it was easy and natural. Now fifty-five and the family patriarch, he felt responsible for his baby brother, Jesús, and he hadn't heard from him in a few days. He went into his home chapel, as he did every day, knelt before the statue of the Virgin Mother, and said the Rosary for his family, his friends, and his business.

He had made many friends in forty years but also plenty of enemies. There was no way the building association would have allowed Alvarez to live in the upper west side penthouse, so he bought the building. He rarely left his

5,000-square-foot fortress, but when he did, it was in his blacked-out bulletproof Cadillac Escalade flanked by another identical vehicle with four armed guards. Time gets away from you when you run an eleven-billion-dollar empire. Alvarez had parlayed protection, loan sharking, drugs, gambling, and more into an international consortium with employees and family in London, Paris, Istanbul, Budapest, Rome, Moscow, and Berlin. It was easier to say where he wasn't connected. He had taken the money from gambling and bought legal casinos; with drug money he purchased fashion houses; with loan sharking funds he now owned banks. But no matter how legitimate he had become, he still had some illegal residue sticking to his shoe, something he liked to keep around to remind him of his roots. Everyone in town knew he had a shady past, but there was no proof, only legend. No one dared to take him on.

Loan sharking was his beginning, but now it was only a small piece of the business. Still, that was why Jesús was sent to Indianapolis—to open a branch. Jesús called every day to keep him posted on how the new work in Indy was doing. He had screwed up so many times in the Big Apple that he had lost the support of other family members. AA had to find a place to send him, to give him something to do. Loan sharking with a bunch of hayseeds seemed right. How could he get in trouble in a sleepy little backwater nicknamed "Nap Town"?

The loan business was now much more sophisticated, focused primarily on sports. It started with a loan to a desperate or enterprising gambler with a history of making good on his debts. The loan, with interest, was due in thirty days. But if the payment was late, the gambler would need some encouragement to pay at least part of the loan back. This was where Jesús came in: he would provide the encouragement. He had gone out to Indy with Antonio Sanchez, one of the meanest, toughest SOBs ever. They were sent out on the company jet, and AA expected reports. He wanted Jesús to do his job, and "please don't kill anyone," he told him with a big hug.

Antonio and Jesús rented a house as their base of operations and started their rounds at the sports bars and clubs where they knew they would meet the right people. They also had an industry network of people who knew who needed funds and were good risks. They particularly wanted to know who bet on the Colts and the Pacers. That was where the big money was to be found.

After two weeks of meeting the typical losers and small-timers, Antonio and Jesús were getting anxious. Jesús, in particular, wanted some good news for his next daily update with AA. They had decided to call it a day and stopped by Buffalo Wild Wings Bar in Broad Ripple.

Tom Clarke sat down at the bar next to them. He had already been drinking. "Hi, boys, you don't look like you're from around here." He had forgotten that Hispanics had moved into central Indiana over the past forty years.

Jesús laughed. "What's your problem?"

Hearing the New York Mexican accent, Clarke gave them the all-knowing evil eye. "I was right, Pedro. You're from the East Coast via Mexico City, right?" Clarke pointed a shaky finger and winked. Through his drunken haze he still could tell these guys could handle themselves. He also knew they were not with the Chamber of Commerce.

Jesús was agitated; it was part of his problem. He was a hothead. He stood up and said, "Back off."

Antonio grabbed his jacket. "Get on the other side of me, now!" That was why Antonio Sanchez had been sent with Jesús, to keep him out of this kind of trouble.

Clarke was cool and felt more alert now. He wasn't scared; he had wiped the floor with many toughs like Jesús.

"Hey, sorry, guys. I'm Tom Clarke, I'm from here. Let's

start over. Tell me about yourselves." Jesús sat down, Clarke leaned back, and Antonio relaxed.

Clarke didn't really want to know much about Jesús and Antonio, which was good because they didn't tell him much. "You're right, we are from New York," said Antonio. "We're here to start a new business."

Clarke winced. "With this economy, good luck. You'll need it." He felt obliged to ask, "What kind of business?"

Antonio smiled. "We're starting a bank."

Clarke laughed out loud. "A bank?" He was incredulous.

Undeterred, Antonio shot back, "Not a normal bank; one for special customers only, a private bank."

Clarke wasn't buying it. "You guys don't look like bankers. What kind of customers get into your private bank?" He waited for an answer.

The second beer had now hit Jesús' cerebral cortex; this was where things usually went wrong. He thought he would move to intimidate his potential client. "The kind that need a lot of money fast, with no collateral, willing to pay high interest, short-term turnaround cash-flow loans."

Clarke thought a minute and then chuckled. "I could use a lot of money real fast. When do you guys open?"

"We're open now," Jesús answered.

Clarke ordered another G and T and started talking about his problems. It looked like an evening for loose tongues and posturing. It was a bitter pill for him to swallow. The trajectory of his life was once so blessed, but now he sounded like a loser as he told two strangers his tale of woe.

✳ ✳ ✳

Tom grew up in New Castle, primarily known as the

hometown of Ray Pavy and Steve Alford, both icons of Indiana high school basketball. Pavy was a once-great player whose career came to a tragic end in a car crash. Well-known in Indiana basketball lore, he would sit in his wheelchair courtside at IU games. Alford played for Bobby Knight, won a national championship, and had a five-year NBA career.

As a student at Butler University, Tom was bright and gifted, an academic star. The harder the subject, the more he relished it. He was at the top of his class all four years at Butler. He was also a devout follower of Christ.

It started for him at a typical revival meeting in his home church on a warm and unusually humid night with poorly sung hymns and downright scary preaching. Lots of talk about hell, where people like him would burn for eternity, surrounded by worms and demons, gnash their teeth, and cry for water forever.

Like many, when he heard the choice of go to hell and spend eternity suffering or go to heaven and enjoy bliss, it was an easy decision. It seemed like a pretty good trade-off. All he had to do was give up Sally Meiter, or at least delay what he dreamed about doing with Sally Meiter. He had spent so many weeks cultivating her that he shook his head over all that wasted time and effort. He made his decision and "crossed Jordan."

Just like the Israelites, Tom had entered the promised land. The downside was that even if he could keep his hands off Sally, he also was expected to keep his hands off himself. This was a bridge too far for him. In his mind, fairness called for him to be able to use what the Baptists called "the right hand of fellowship." Still, by the time he got to Butler, he was not only a staunch believer, he was eager to convert others. He was not the stereotypical enthusiastic advocate you could stump with a few good questions. He was an expert apologist for the faith.

When he met Michael Hart at a Butler basketball game in the famed Hinkle Fieldhouse, they hit it off and decided to do a post-game autopsy on the Bulldogs' loss at Steak and Shake. Michael and Tom were both on academic full rides, Hart in molecular biology and Clarke in physics; they were in the same chemistry class. They both enjoyed philosophy, science, and history.

Michael was a typical Catholic, a product of absolution without repentance. He went to mass every Sunday to confess his sins, take the magic pill, and drink the blood to cleanse him so he could go out and repeat the same sins until the next Sunday. Clarke was convinced Michael didn't have a clue about what a real Christian would be, a follower of Christ 24/7.

The conversation that started Michael on his journey to becoming the Reverend Michael Hart began that night. Clarke looked him straight in the eye and said, "Michael, do you really believe in the pope?"

Michael was a bit surprised, "Not really. The history on that isn't too clear to me." He sighed, "Popes aren't too good of an idea. They suddenly became celibate in the Middle Ages. Funny how it worked out...no sons, but many nephews. Oh well, like I said, bad idea."

Clarke decided to drill deeper. "Michael, what do you think a true Christian is?"

"Listen, man, I know what you're trying to do—get me to become a Baptist like you."

"Not really," Clarke retorted. "I want to peel this down to the core. What does it mean to be a Christian, a follower of Christ?"

"Okay." Michael laughed. "Accept Jesus Christ as my Lord and Savior, all right? Does that make you happy, is that the right answer, will you now shut up and let me eat?"

It didn't seem like a good start, but for Michael and Clarke it was. They loved to argue about everything, and they did so for the next year. At length, Michael decided that what it meant to be a Christian was pretty simple: to put his confidence in Jesus Christ, to believe that Jesus existed, was God incarnate, did die for the sins of the world, and did rise from the dead, and that Jesus was not only his God but his leader. He decided to follow Jesus every day. He especially liked to think of himself as a disciple of Christ, learning from Him how to live his live as though Jesus were living it.

Michael and Clarke became a force to be reckoned with on the Butler campus, in fact with anyone who ever met up with them. Not only were they aggressive; they were smart and well studied. The typical objections used by skeptics to fend off Christians didn't work; they cut through them like a hot knife through warm butter. People would bring up problems with the Bible, the hypocrisy of the church, the Crusades, the Inquisition, and televangelism, and the two would destroy every argument. Even their professors avoided the normal digs against religion, because they knew they would have their hands full and more than likely be made to look like ignorant fools.

They both graduated with highest honors. The year was 1994, and both men were recruited by several national firms. In a radical departure from the norm, they both joined the Navy. After Officer Candidate School and Naval Intelligence School, they went their separate ways.

Clarke's genius was evident. His ability to handle complicated data and to be focused and disciplined in difficult moments immediately caught the attention of the Special Forces. He was taken aside and given additional training and spent the next ten years in covert work. He emerged a different man—still religious but more acquainted with his dark side and the underbelly of life. He learned to be disciplined when it was needed and to let himself blow a gasket when discipline wasn't needed.

As big as his gifts were, his weaknesses were their equal. He drank too much; he gambled in search of a high, a win, a rush. His life was too high-octane for Mary and Janis, his ex-wives, and for Peggy, Rhonda, Joy, and other victims to be named later. Clarke couldn't do the ordinary, the common, the mundane, the regular. He found life unlivable. He was brilliant, depressed, and broke.

He did have plans to turn his life around; he had even reconnected all these years later with Michael, who had become a celebrity Christian. He trusted Michael and was trying to find his old self, the one who led his pastor friend to Christ. After spending only one lunch with him, he felt he was making progress. But this night, once again, he was hanging out in a bar, trolling for another nameless friend, someone who would listen to his stories about Navy SEAL stuff. It used to be secret what guys like Clarke did, but now there were movies, books, and documentaries. They even knew what kind of techniques they used and the nature of the equipment. *Why not use it for what I need?* Clarke reasoned through the alcoholic blubber.

This is what happens when you drink too much. Instead of talking to some potential creature of pleasure, I'm talking to two half-drunk tatted Mexicans from New York who think they own a bank.

He decided to put them to the test. "All right, I need fifty grand tomorrow. Where do I meet you to get it?" He waited with the award-winning smile that had gotten him so much in life.

Jesús calmly asked, "What do you have for collateral? 'Cause we don't want to have to break your knees, asshole."

Clarke frowned. "Come on, boys, you really have fifty big ones?"

"Yeah," Jesús said, "you can have it now if you want, but you will need to sign a contract."

Clarke smiled. "Where is the contract?

Jesús scribbled on a Buffalo Wings napkin and shoved it across the bar. "You owe me fifty k plus 20 percent interest thirty days from now." Jesús scrawled the date 9/17/12, signed his name, and slammed down the pen.

Clarke thought, *I could pay the child support, the alimony, and my back rent, and if a few games break my way, I can do this.* He reached for the pen.

— 3 —
CINCINNATI

How Clarke got Michael into it was baffling, but no mystery. After the First Bank of You Better Pay Back on Time with 20 percent Monthly Interest or We Will Break Your Legs issued the loan, Clarke was broke. He lost all but ten thousand on his bets with the thirty thousand he used to parlay into sixty thousand he needed to repay Jesús. The rest of the money went to alimony for his ex-wives and child support for his daughter.

Clarke was pretty good at hiding. He was trained to hide, and he avoided Jesús and Antonio for two weeks as they frantically tried to find him. They finally caught up with him at a Kroger's in the frozen food section. He was pulling six Morton's TV dinners from the freezer when Jesús slammed the glass door on his arm.

"Hey, Tommy Boy," he growled, "we've been looking for you." He seemed to enjoy torturing those who couldn't pay more than collecting from those who could.

The Morton's dinners scattered across the floor, and Clarke grabbed Jesús by the throat and had him screaming in pain as he was forced to his knees. "Real tough guy, aren't you?" Clarke said with a grim chuckle. "I've killed dozens like you. Never touch me again!"

An embarrassed Jesús bounced off the floor, but Antonio grabbed him, held him back with one arm's incredible strength, and got between the two. "We will give you one more day to come up with the money," he said. "You won't like what happens if you don't." Antonio kept a good grip on Jesús, and they left the store.

*　*　*

Michael would never forget the next day because it happened to be the day he and Clarke were driving to Cincinnati to see a Reds game. Both were lifelong Reds fans. They were too young to remember much about the Big Red Machine, the days of Pete Rose, Joe Morgan, Johnny Bench, Tony Perez, and company, but still to them they were legends. The team these days was lackluster in comparison, but much improved ever since signing Joey Votto and Neftali Soto and with the managerial expertise of Dusty Baker. The fans were upbeat.

As they left Indianapolis for the ninety-mile drive to Riverfront Stadium, Michael noticed a car always in the rearview mirror. Sometimes it was right behind them, other times a car or two back, but the white Escalade was always there. Sometimes these things could be coincidental. Michael had no reason to believe anyone would follow a pastor and parishioner to a baseball game.

It began to concern him, however, when he saw two men watching them at the concession where he and Clarke were buying mid-game hot dogs. "Hey, Tom, do you see those two Hispanics at four o'clock?"

Clarke had been trying to forget his problems. Much of the discussion in the car had dealt with his asking Michael how to break the power of some of his addictions. They had few secrets from each other, but Antonio and Jesús were one. Clarke didn't want to look, knowing who it must be. He turned and saw the two loan sharks sipping their beers.

"Yeah, what about them?" He wanted to seem blasé.

"They are either awfully interested in us, or we have a lot of common interests." Michael went on, "They don't have seats near us, but they stood in the exit near us for the first five innings. When I went to the men's room, they were there; when I got popcorn, they were there. Now we get hot dogs, and here they are again. We are under surveillance, not very good surveillance, but still, surveillance."

Clarke looked away. "I wouldn't worry about it. Once an operator, always an operator. Relax, you're not in Bosnia anymore."

Michael put the two out of his mind. He enjoyed the Reds' comeback in the bottom of the eighth, and they held on for a victory. It was almost like the glory days. Michael just stood and enjoyed the beauty of the field before departing the stadium.

Michael and Clarke were almost to their car when Antonio and Jesús caught up with them. Clearly they thought it would be a good idea to make a point out in the dark parking lot. Michael saw them coming, and instinct told him, *bad guys*. He turned just as both of them went to the passenger side of the car and grabbed Clarke.

"Time to pay, Tommy Boy," said Jesús as he hit Clarke with what looked like a Little League baseball bat. Clarke was surprised, and the bat hit him square on the right shoulder. Antonio grabbed him so Jesús could hit him again. Before Michael could get there, Clarke took blows to the head and right knee as he struggled to protect himself.

Normally friends and bystanders don't interfere when a weapon is involved, so the two ignored Michael until Antonio felt excruciating pain in his neck. Michael had his thumb on that special place that makes people drop to their knees. He chopped down on Antonio's neck once more, and the big man slumped to the ground, out cold.

Clarke finally kicked Jesús off him, slamming him against the Lexus next to them. Just as Jesús bounced back, Michael met him with the heel of his hand under the chin. Jesús screamed in pain as he bit through his tongue. He fell to his knees against the white Lexus, clutching his face. Seeing the blood in his hands, he was unable to do anything but pass out. He slid down the side of the car, smearing blood everywhere.

By this time, a few heads were popping up from surrounding cars. Michael told Clarke, "Get in." They soon disappeared into the natural flow of traffic. In ten minutes, they were headed northwest on Interstate 74 back to Indy. Still stunned, Antonio and Jesús somehow scrambled away before security was called.

The scuffle was reported by stadium police as an "altercation over undisclosed issues with minor injuries to the assailants." No one bothered to get a number off the Indiana plates. The car was described as a dark, late model sedan—a Honda or Toyota, possibly a BMW. "They all kinda look the same," the only witness was willing to say.

It was painfully obvious to those who caught a glimpse of the fight that this was one to stay away from. It was not some sloppy drunks swinging at one another but quick, precise, efficient, and sobering. One bystander whispered to his wife, "I thought I was watching Jason Bourne."

"What the hell was that?" Michael said as he slammed the steering wheel. "What have you done now, Tom? You've come back to church, we're spending time together, you're reading Scripture. I thought you were serious about change."

Clarke slumped in the seat. "I owe them money."

Michael sighed. "How much?"

Clarke moaned. "Oh, over fifty large. I can't believe I did it; I was drunk when I met them." He poured out the rest of his story.

Michael knew it all, the ex-wives, the wasted years the locusts ate, the addiction to desire, the life of the body being the master. His mind was racing. "Where are those guys from? Did you say New York City?"

"Yes, at least that's where they said they were from." Clarke didn't want to reveal more.

Michael was thinking out loud, "You know they work for somebody; idiots like that don't have their own money. Whoever is behind them will send in the first team to get the money, because those guys are flunkies.

"Tom, how could you?" He was picking up steam. "I'm a pastor, I have a family, I'm responsible for many people and for the reputation of Christ in my community." He shook his head. "I just rang up a couple of thugs in the Reds parking lot. They probably have my license number. We'll be hearing from the police unless we're very lucky."

Michael knew that even if the police didn't find them, the two guys they hammered would.

※　※　※

For several weeks he lived with the growing realization that he was in danger. He knew well that Jen, Corey, and Janie could be threatened. His church, his entire career, could be destroyed. It became harder to concentrate on his daily work.

And praying—what do you pray? "Lord, send them away. Lord, take them out. Lord, take Tom out of my life." It was too late to pray it would all go away. Now the Mexican Mafia wanted revenge. He pondered all this as he stared out of the Starbucks window. Thirty minutes passed as his mind fixed on the problem, running scenarios. Just then Frank Ewald came through the door, snapping him back to the present.

Frank sat down in the crowded shop next to Michael. Michael preferred to have something pleasant to drink when he was doing something unpleasant. Starbucks looked hip, nonreligious; it represented the real world to Michael. Sitting beside Frank Ewald was like being in the presence of a musty hymnal.

Ewald looked up from his tall coffee of the day. "I can't believe people spend this much for coffee! Think of how much could be used for God's work." He almost snorted in disgust.

Frank looked like he'd just walked off the pages of the 1962 J. C. Penney catalogue. He wore a dark brown shirt, a tan sports coat, beige polyester slacks with matching socks, and brown shoes—the baron of brown. He represented much of what was wrong with American Christianity: a lust for power and an angry spirit. He was the kind of man who had a clean garage and a dirty mind. Thankfully, the mocha latte would keep Michael from gagging. There were no courses in seminary on the Frank Ewalds of the church. Most professors didn't talk about him because they didn't know about him.

"I don't know why we have to meet here," barked Ewald. "Don't we provide you with a nice office?"

There he goes again, thought Michael. *He thinks he provides it, that he owns it. Doesn't he realize I started this church from scratch, and he is just one of thousand?* He smiled. "I feel comfortable here, and nobody really hears us or cares about our discussion."

"Michael." Ewald leaned into Michael's private space, suffusing him with ghoulish breath. "You have great influence in this city, and God wants you to be a good steward of that power. It's time. For such a time as this you have been called. You need to stand like the watchman on the wall warning this country about its moral collapse and the impending danger of God's discipline. He is about to write 'Ichabod, the glory has departed,' over the doorposts of this once great land!"

Ewald leaned back, finally having had his say. Just like his friends told him he should, speak truth to power.

Michael had made the decision many times: he would not get publicly involved in politics. It would limit his reach into too many lives. His priority was to be able to meet people on a deeper level than their vote. He believed some candidates were more in agreement with his world-view, but he would simply teach the truth from Scripture and allow citizen followers of Jesus to sort out their politics.

"Frank"—this time Michael leaned into Ewald's space—"I will simply repeat here what I have said many times. I am anti-abortion, I preach a commitment to life, and I am against pornography. I do have opinions, and I do vote. I will not march. I will not endorse candidates. I will not sign petitions. That is for you to do, not me."

He continued, "I'm not sure you'd want me to go public. I'm not clear that we did the right thing going into Iraq, I'm probably against the death penalty, and I don't think every person with a valid driver's license should own a gun." He leaned back.

Ewald pursed his lips, and his neck seemed to swell like it was trying to escape the tie around his tight collar. He patted his comb-over carefully, so as not to disturb its dubious structure. He was stunned—not that Michael wouldn't go public, but that such absolute political heresy had just come from his young pastor's mouth.

Frank Ewald stood. "Michael, you've given me much to think about. I will pray and decide if Emma and I can continue in the church. We have many friends who will be distressed by this news. I need to go now."

Michael nodded as Ewald disappeared out the door. He walked fast for a sixty-five-year-old. Michael was sure he would be burning up his rollover minutes getting the word out. It would probably create another meeting; he was sure it would, it always did. When angry people didn't get their way, they lied a lot.

Michael wondered, *Where do people learn to think that way? Where do they come from? What kind of spirituality is that?* He was sure there was a special school somewhere, and Lucifer was the dean. Its specialty was to teach people to be angry, hostile, judgmental troublemakers; if he could find it, he would blow it up. The problem was that the factory for such things was the human heart.

This was Michael's world, a tense, frustrating enterprise of managing mission, motive, and his own emotions. Nothing made him angrier than people wasting his time. Frank Ewald was a time waster. He never came to Michael for pastoral counsel or spiritual direction. It was always to use Michael's influence and position to further his political agenda. Ewald had influence with the over-sixty crowd, which was substantial. There were hundreds of good, serious followers of Christ who gave generously to the church and world missions. These people had time on their hands. Many used to run things: businesses, organizations, and missional endeavors. Often they were easily led by the most vocal or focused among them, and Ewald was that person. One way Michael could protect his flock was to manage Frank Ewald, but most of the time he simply hoped he would go away.

Churches everywhere were full of people who had never been seriously invited to lay aside personal agendas and follow Christ. His church was different; that was his message, that was what he did. Like most pastors, he felt that if people would just "follow what I am teaching," they could live lives of humility, submission, obedience, and sacrifice. They would be very happy, the world would be a better place, and they could replace gossip with joy, slander with loving actions, and boredom with purpose.

Aw, piss on it! He threw away what was left of his latte and headed for his car. Sometimes he wondered whose disciple he was.

One thing Michael missed was driving fast. Whipping through the tight city streets of Prague at 60 miles per hour or through the German countryside at over 100 had been one of his special talents during his younger days, but pastors can't speed. Too many tickets, bad publicity, so he slowly cruised home in his Honda Accord coupe, the perfect clergy-mobile. He didn't notice the white Escalade trailing him as he turned off 465 onto 82nd Street toward his home near Geist Reservoir. Church work had been very good to Jen and Michael. They had gotten a great deal on a very expensive home only a few miles from the church. The gate opened to his drive, and he cruised into the garage. The door came down, and Michael, lost in his thoughts, never saw Antonio and Jesús as they simply noted where he lived and continued through the neighborhood.

Janie leapt into Michael's arms. "Daddy, it's Friday, no school tomorrow! Pizza night!" She wriggled to get down and laughed as Michael feigned chasing after her. Friday nights the pressure was off. Everyone stayed up late, no one had to cook—it was date night. The gleam in Jen's eyes told Michael game on.

As they gobbled up "The Works" from Pizza Hut, the big news was that Corey had escorted the cutest girl in class to the school bus, and they sat together on the way home. They planned to do it again all next week. Jen and Michael tried to show the appropriate delight at the good news but checked each other with a glance, not knowing what to make of this. Michael was thinking twelve was a bit young for a steady girlfriend, and riding the bus home together was…a date! Besides, it was the pastor's son who was doing this at the school that was part of the pastor's church. Big news in the junior high set.

Michael waited until after dinner to say something. "Corey, my boy, let's talk about this girl."

Corey looked uncomfortable, "Okay, why?"

"Her name is Janet, is that what you said?" Michael was using his most understanding voice.

"Yeah," Corey said, looking for the remote, "Janet

Johnson. You probably know her parents."

Michael's mental card file was flipping fast, "I think I do. I'll look them up on our website directory later." Michael thought that was enough, he didn't want to venture too far into Corey's private world. Pressing too hard wouldn't get him invited back. He'd always believed what Jonathan Edwards said, that "every family is a little church and your children are your first disciples." It was ironic to Michael that he had so much knowledge on how to disciple people but rarely knew what to say to Corey. He, too, like most of the parents in his church, relied on the youth pastors to teach his children. Jen and the kids had busy lives, and Friday nights were the best, with no church tomorrow, no school, just fun stuff.

The big drama of the night was Corey's new friend. At least this was what Jen, Corey, and Janie thought. However, after a very satisfying "date" with Jen, Michael couldn't sleep, wondering how long it would be before Tommy would resurface, before more thugs would enter their lives. How much longer would it be safe for either of his kids to ride home on the bus or for Jen to go grocery shopping or have lunch with her friends? He didn't know, but he suspected not long.

— 4 —

Jesús and Antonio were not sure what to do. Befuddlement came naturally to both. Clarke was missing; should they keep looking for him? Luckily, Michael Hart had been easy to find because his face was on a billboard on North Meridian Street. There were ten such billboards on the north side of Marion County inviting people to join The Challenge; "Change your life, Change the world." They had cruised through the church parking lot, and when they saw the car from Riverfront Stadium parked in the pastor's spot, they knew they had their man. When you get your face smashed and spend a few days in pain, you tend to remember where it happened and some of the details.

※　※　※

Jesús still didn't know what to do. He wanted his money, but he also wanted revenge. He decided to call Alonzo, who answered his phone from a suite at the Gresham Palace Four Seasons Hotel in Budapest.

Alonzo liked to walk out on a balcony when he talked business. It was safer, harder to hear on electronic listening devices. He stood overlooking the famous Danube River and the Chain Bridge. The suite was $5,000 US a night, but it was worth it because he believed that if there was something more important than being rich, it was looking rich. Alonzo Alvarez covered both bases.

Budapest was Alonzo's door to Eastern Europe and the former Soviet Republics, where he did business. Here he held court as his many suppliers visited him in the suite, groveling, reporting, and negotiating. It was early evening in Budapest. Alvarez was preparing for an evening of entertaining his guests. Nothing was out of his reach; the best women and wine were his. For this evening he had rented a private palace on Margaret Island. It was expected that they would not leave the palace until dawn. An early morning stroll on the island, down the waterfront, past Parliament, to the hotel always invigorated Alonzo.

"Little brother," Alonzo said affectionately. He couldn't erase the memories of little Jesús running naked around his house so many years ago. "There must be a reason for your call." He walked back into the room and motioned to his valet for his shirt.

Jesús was slow to speak. "We've got this guy who owes us sixty large, can't find him right now, but we found his friend, and—"

"And what?" Alonzo interrupted. In his gut he knew Jesús had screwed up again. "So what's the problem?"

"He's a priest, you know, they call them preachers, and he's famous. At least he's up on billboards around this town."

"What the hell does a preacher have to do with this? Why are you following him?"

"Because he rung up me and Antonio." Jesús sounded pathetic.

Alonzo was laughing now. "So let me get this straight: a preacher beat the shit out of the both of you? How is that possible?"

Jesús took a deep breath. "He knows martial arts. He hurt us fast, and we were out. So we came back to Indy to look for the guy who owes us the money, and we saw the pastor's face on the billboard, and we went to his church and followed him home. We know where he lives, and I'm sure he knows where we can find this guy who owes us."

Alonzo paused for a moment. "All right, keep following the preacher. You call that cop we pay; his name is Bohannon, Kenny Bohannon. I will send him a message, and he'll look up this pastor and get personal information. What's the debtor's name?" The valet was now taking notes.

"Tom Clarke," Jesús said.

"Get his address from Bohannon too. That's what we pay him for. Call me back if you don't get this fixed!"

Alonzo pressed end call; enough of little brother for today. With that, the valet helped him slip on his evening jacket, and security escorted him to the elevator and down to his waiting town car. He considered that at night, with its bridges and palaces spangled with light, the Danube was one of the great wonders of the world. The car slipped quietly across the Margaret Bridge and onto the island for an elegant night of debauchery. There would be many women, tasty cuisine, and many guards with weapons tucked beneath designer suits tailored for such occasions. It was Alonzo's idea of a fund-raiser: "give or else."

*　*　*

Bohannon looked down at his phone—a blocked number, and all the text said was "Expect a call."

Kenny knew something was up. He rarely got this kind of message and knew it was from Alonzo. Five minutes later his phone rang.

"This is Jesús. My brother told you to expect a call; this is it."

"Hey, Jesús, what can I do you for?"

"I need to know about two people. The first is Tom Clarke; he lives here in Indy. The second is a preacher, Michael Hart. His church is called The Challenge; Change your Life, Change the World." Jesús didn't know the difference between a name and a motto.

When he heard Hart's name, Bohannon laughed. "Why do you wanna know about him? He's a local pastor on the northeast side."

"Don't worry about it. Just give it to me." Jesús was getting mad.

"Awright, back off. I'll get back to ya in a couple hours."

Thirty minutes later Bohannon was done, and he was surprised. He couldn't figure out why Jesús would need to know about a couple of guys who were straight arrows. Clarke was a graduate of Butler University with a seven-year career in Navy Intelligence and two divorces. But hey, he thought, a life in law enforcement leads to divorce; his monthly alimony check proved that. The only possibility was that Clarke borrowed money, but why would he borrow it from Jesús? In a word, desperation. He had Clarke's phone and address, 6124 Broadway in Broad Ripple, and he would send them soon.

Michael Hart, however, made no sense. He was famous, well paid, and pastor of the biggest and most successful church on the north side of Indianapolis. There was no way he borrowed money; this ought to prove interesting.

The Challenge was where his ex-wife and his two sons, Jerry and Franky, went to church and also where the boys went to grade school. He had been there a couple of times for school events. He leaned back and remembered that Jerry had spent the night a couple of times at the Hart home, birthday sleepovers or something.

Everyone loved Michael Hart. He looked clean as a whistle, but Kenny ran a background check on him anyway. Something else was interesting: Hart had also been in the Navy during roughly the same years as Clarke. All Clarke's and Hart's specific military records were classified, not available to a local police officer. Two Butler grads at the top of their class, recruited by the Navy, and disappeared for several years. It was obvious that they had known each other for a very long time.

Two hours later, as promised, Bohannon called Jesús

back. "I've got some information." He passed along the data and then added, "Looks like the pastor and Clarke have been friends since college. Both were in the Navy at the same time, and their records are sealed, probably Special Ops."

This made some sense to Jesús and Antonio, even though sense was not something either had in abundance.

"I'd be careful with these guys," Bohannon warned, "especially the pastor. You want headlines? You mess with him, there will be headlines."

✳ ✳ ✳

Michael was back in the office early Sunday morning preparing for the first of three services. His ritual was a stop by Starbucks for the Venti Americano and plain butter croissant they always reserved for him. He loved that first sip and bite together as he began to review his edits from the Saturday night services. It was one of life's important little pleasures.

Five services in less than twenty-four hours took a lot out of him, but for this he was born. He had more on his plate than the sermon. Always there was fear—when would the other shoe fall? He had learned years ago how to wall off wandering thoughts and fears. That skill served him well, especially when the most intense mental requirements of the week were upon him—writing and delivering a sermon to thousands. His sermon would be edited and televised in over sixty countries and heard by thousands more via a weekly podcast. His assistants cherry-picked his most pithy quotes and tweeted them to over 400,000 followers on Twitter.

Michael's sermon was about the real divide in the country. He called the series *A World Split Apart*. He'd named it after Alexander Solzhenitsyn's courageous and controversial speech at Harvard on June 8, 1978. Because it was translated live from Russian into English, many in attendance were slow to understand its implications.

The "split" Solzhenitsyn spoke of was easily illustrated by the difference between the traditional understanding of freedom and the secular humanistic point of view. Solzhenitsyn scolded the professors and elites in attendance for abandoning the biblical worldview, which is freedom to advance what is morally good. The secular view is freedom from restriction. Freedom, Solzhenitsyn explained, has always been for the advancement of a moral good: to serve others, to live for others. The freedom championed by the secular community is freedom from any moral restrictions, freedom to commit unlimited abortions, to engage in lust and pornography, to pursue only selfish interests. This, of course, drew some boos from the august crowd.

Solzhenitsyn brought his argument to a powerful conclusion: "There are many who would like to find evil in the world and destroy it. But the line between good and evil runs through the human heart, and who is willing to destroy himself?"

This was a serious subject, and Michael had to be careful, but he depended on his methodical, extensive preparation and his discipline to state his points with precision. Those days in training when he was tortured and waterboarded—and kept in a cage for over twenty hours tormented by continuous streams of heavy metal music—had taught him how to focus his mind and even play tricks on himself to fight the emotions that betrayed normal men. It didn't hurt that four years in seminary taught him how to study, meditate, think, and write. Then he put his pop culture hat on and displayed his degree from the Mary Poppins school of preaching: "a spoonful of sugar makes the medicine go down."

Michael's factory-installed smile, his Robert Redford looks, and his off-the-wall humor made him easy to look at and listen to. He was special. He could scold you, teach you, make you laugh till it hurt and cry until you had no more tears. But it was never easy. It took hard work, and Michael relished it all.

As he prayed, it troubled him that he had hurt those men. He begged God to send them away. He didn't want to be reminded of those days. It had taken him years to bury the memories of the horror of Bosnia, the many nights he plunged a knife into unsuspecting souls and sent them into eternity. Where did they go? Did their souls live with God, or had he sent them to an eternal grave? His entire life now was about saving souls and attending to those in pain. He had killed so many; he had created so much pain. His inner struggle was starting again, the past beginning to haunt him once more. Whose disciple was he really, when it came down to it?

Michael walked into the sanctuary, the service already in progress. Every eye followed him as he sat, laid down his Bible, and lifted his hands to join the singing. Beside him sat Jen, who preferred the Sunday morning 8:00 service. She put her arm around Michael's waist, a way to say good morning without speaking. Corey and Janie were there, Corey barely awake, Janie perky and ready to go.

It was later, during the 9:30 service, that Michael noticed his special visitors. There they were, Jesús and Antonio, seated on the aisle five rows back, taking it all in. Michael thought they might take it all in and repent, but even he was not that optimistic. Between services they disappeared. For some reason they didn't hang around for coffee and rolls. It was clear to him that they had found him, and it was game on. He thought immediately about Jen and the kids.

At the 11:00 service he caught a glimpse of Tom Clarke.

This was the first time he had surfaced in a couple of weeks. It was a good thing that Clarke had not been spotted by Jesús and Antonio in the lobby.

By the time Michael got home, it was 1:30. Jen had lunch ready, but Corey wasn't there. "Where is Corey?" Michael asked with uncommon intensity in his voice.

"Oh, he went to that nice boy's house, Jerry Bohannon. I really like Sally and her boys."

Michael thought a moment. "Okay, that sounds all right."

— 5 —

Even though Michael was a pastoral superstar and community luminary, some of his life was ordinary and even dull. Part of that dullness was a monthly church council meeting. Tonight was that night: a pot of chili and a few hours of conversation with those to whom he was accountable.

Michael was very powerful; no one had the clout to rein him in. It was something he had to choose to be in his life. He believed that submission to these nine men was a way that God could meet his needs; it was a way to keep him on track. After all, when a famous person falls from grace, everyone says, "He wasn't accountable to anyone." Michael was determined that would never be said of him.

He looked around the room as the men ate the chili, some liking Fritos and cheese on top, others opting for the cornbread. They laughed, joked, and talked—mostly about the upcoming Colts season and what they thought of their number one draft pick, Andrew Luck. Michael's most trusted friend here was Ron Walker, a forty-seven-year-old personal injury attorney Michael had introduced to Christ within a week after they met ten years ago. He was rich and well known in Marion County, with a huge estate on Geist Reservoir. Walker had defended several infamous clients, let's say of questionable character, but also many true victims and spent many an hour on Court TV.

Ron had leaned on Michael a great deal when his oldest son was arrested for a DUI; that was the time when they truly bonded. Now that Ron's two sons were at Purdue and his only daughter was a senior at a private school, he had the time to give leadership to the council. Michael's and Ron's families had vacationed together, and they were tight.

There was complete trust.

This was what Michael wanted for all his leaders: to engage in relationships of trust based on integrity. It was core to Michael's teaching that the most important question that could be asked of another person is "Can I trust me with you?" This meant that whatever there was to know about a person could be known by at least one other person.

This was what Michael really believed, but he found that he could not practice it himself. He had partitioned off his secret life; somehow he had rationalized that this principle of full disclosure didn't apply to his military days. He was sworn to secrecy by law and was not free to tell anyone. Ron didn't know this about his best friend; Jen didn't know it about the man she slept with every night. Until recently, that man, that person, had been dead and gone. Then in that parking lot in Cincinnati, he jumped out of Michael's body and took over, having been there all the time. He was beginning to think like the apostle Paul: "I don't really understand myself, for I want to do what is right, but I don't do it. Instead, I do what I hate." It was within the secret compartment of his soul that Michael doubted his own teaching: *Can people really change?* He was confused.

Ron Walker called the meeting to order. "Great sermon today, Michael. I never thought I would know anything about a Russian novelist named Solzhenitsyn or feel downright educated." Walker smirked as the entire room erupted with laughter.

Michael smiled. "There will be a spelling test next week on long Russian names."

The meeting was normal. They discussed the new high school building. The capital fund-raising plan was about at an end; just another $500,000 was needed to completely pay for it. There was confidence in the room that a few people sitting here could pick up the slack.

Ron and Michael had privately discussed a sabbatical policy for the staff. The church was not yet ten years old. Some of the staff had been there seven years, and it was believed in order to keep the good ones, continued education, rest, and reflection should be afforded to the most faithful staff. That was to begin with Michael himself, right after Christmas.

"Michael, could you explain to the council why any pastor would need three months off with pay?"

"Men, you know that the pastoral life is 24/7. It requires all of you, all of the time. Every seven years I believe we need unfettered time for rest, reflection, and journaling or writing. This will lead to a better pastor, a better person, a better church." Michael smiled and leaned back.

Jim Carlson cleared his throat. "Michael, I've run my own business for over thirty years now. I've never taken that much time off at once, and I certainly don't expect to get paid. The staff already have paid vacation. I just don't like it!" Carlson's voice was quivering by the time he finished.

The room was quiet; not many had taken on Michael so directly, and it was hard for him. It made his decade of hard work, of starting this entire organization from scratch, seem unappreciated. Jim Carlson wasn't a crusty curmudgeon like Frank Ewald, but they were both from the old school. People like that couldn't seem to understand the difference between building houses and building a church.

Michael moved forward with caution: "Jim, the pastoral life is primarily, by nature, a spiritually directed one. I would submit to you that a three-month sabbatical is not three months off, but three months of focusing on the very issues that create a higher spirituality. It is work, Jim, a spiritual building if you will." Jim didn't quite get it, but he did get it that Michael was convinced.

"All right, Michael," Jim said with a sigh. "You're no slouch. I don't think you will be sunning yourself on South

Beach in Miami or riding yourself silly at Disney World. Go for it, and report back to us."

It was a bit irritating that Jim seemed to think he was the one approving the motion. Michael knew that Jim Carlson represented hundreds of his congregation, hard-working, independent Hoosiers who still believed that the Indiana High School Basketball Association should never have allowed schools to be divided into classifications. They longed for the old days when Milan won the state tourney depicted in the film *Hoosiers*. Michael knew that no matter how big you became in the public arena, the Jim Carlsons of the world would watch over your soul, even though they thought they were keeping you in line. Those might even be the same thing.

On the way out the door, Ron stopped Michael. "Guess you got that sabbatical, but not without some pushback."

"Yeah." Michael smiled. "Just don't know when I will have time to take it."

Ron looked at Michael sideways, skeptical. "Now look whose dauber is down. Is something wrong? We need to get together."

Michael paused. "I'm all right. When do you want to meet?"

Three days later Michael and Ron sat at Michael's favorite Starbucks at the corner of Broad Ripple Avenue and Guilford. It was far enough away from church that they didn't get interrupted much.

One of Michael's favorite sayings was "People are accountable only to the level of their honesty." This haunted him as he looked at Ron across the table. He had never considered before that he was hiding anything from Ron, but now he was deeply convicted that he was. This was a crisis moment for him. *Do I really trust my friend? Do I really mean what I say? Is Michael Hart a man of integrity?*

Ron was a funny man, always ready with a joke or story. Too often he would blurt something out in a meeting that was obviously unplanned. Michael remembered the time in the early days when two pastors and their spouses came to visit the church because they wanted to know what made The Challenge such a success. Ron was involved in many of the innovative small groups that he and Michael had designed.

Ron tended to get excited, and he began to explain it to the two couples by saying, "I tell you what, when you get someone excited like that, before you know it, you're 'in their pants,' and they're sold." The women both blushed, the husbands laughed, and Michael fell out of his chair laughing.

They had been through a lot together, but Ron got lied to for a living. He was an expert on lying, and Michael was unsure what to do.

Ron took it down to a whisper. "So what's bothering you?"

"Ah, I don't really know, Ron. I'm not sleeping well, but everything seems okay at home. Maybe it's the stress of the funding needs, the endless requests for my time, I'm just not clear." He took a sip of his latte, not sure if Ron would stop.

True to form, Ron raised his voice. "Come on, Michael. You're not talking to the church board now. This is not a cover story with the Indianapolis Star. It's me, man, your confidant." Ron was pushing. "There is something you're not telling me, I can feel it. Are you having an affair? Did you steal money, do you have a gambling habit, are you addicted to porn? Tell me, I can handle it!"

Ron was peering at him now. "You know, you taught us what Bonhoeffer said, that your sin wants to be alone with you. You've taught me that as soon as you turn the light on the problem and let another person in on your secret, it destroys sin's grip on you. It runs like a cockroach when the lights are turned on." Ron leaned back, frustrated

Michael simply looked at him. "I can tell you this, Ron. It's nothing you've mentioned. In fact, it's nothing at all. I'll just need to sort this out myself."

He knew this was a watershed moment in his relationship to his best friend; he had just lied. He thought, however, that if the truth ever came out someday, Ron would forgive him. But watching a disappointed Ron leave the building, he knew it would never be the same between them. He had breached the bond of trust between them, even though he didn't think there was any other way he could have done it. If he had told the truth, Ron, as an officer of the court, would be subject to censure. He would also want to help, and this would endanger him, as well as putting his wife, two sons, and daughter in jeopardy.

— 6 —

The day started quite normally as they saw the kids onto the bus. They only drove them to school when they were running late. Corey and Janie loved to ride the bus. It made them feel normal, part of the gang, not members of religious royalty being ferried to school by the Daddy-King.

Thirty minutes with Millie caught Michael up on his schedule and the important gossip. Wednesday afternoon would begin Michael's reading and study time, which extended through Thursday. This was the engine room of his soul. It was what made everything work for him. He was reading *Bad Religion: How We Became a Nation of Heretics*, by Ross Douthat, a critique of how individualism had fractured much of evangelicalism. He particularly liked a passage on page 231:

"Religious man was made to be saved, but psychological man was made to be pleased."

He thought this would be great to include in his World Split Apart series. The theological–psychological split was part of the larger cultural split. He was struggling through historian Paul Johnson's *Modern Times*, over a thousand pages of very small print, but a better history of the world since 1900 could not be found. But before he submerged himself into the world of thought and ideas, he would need to meet with Lisa Rathbone.

❋   ❋   ❋

Lisa was 5-9, twenty-nine, and 109. She was somehow able to pour herself into the dresses she wore, though no one was sure how. She dressed for a counseling appointment as if she was on her way to a Paris fashion show along the Champs-Elysées. Her hair was spiked in an interesting but confusing way. Her sunglasses, which she never removed, made Michael's Pradas look lowbrow.

Michael's counseling policy was to see someone no more than three times and then make a referral. This was appointment three, and Michael wasn't sure if he wanted it to end or not. He knew it needed to end for his own good. He had already seen too much of Mrs. Rathbone, every time she tried to sit down on the couch in a dress especially created for R-rated viewing at such a moment. She was very rich, very unhappy, and very dangerous.

Michael often thought of a wise proverb when he met with Mrs. Rathbone, the one that said, "Wisdom will save you from the immoral woman, from the seductive words of the promiscuous woman. She has abandoned her husband and ignores the covenant she made before God. Entering her house leads to death; it is the road to the grave. The man who visits her is doomed."

"I'm just a piece of meat to him," Mrs. Rathbone said with her fake European accent. No linguist could trace it, because it came from nowhere, unless you consider an insecure girl's troubled mind to be somewhere.

Him referred to her husband, Elmore Rathbone; his family had immigrated to the United States in the early twentieth century and made their way to Indiana. The Rathbones had established a chain of department stores in the upper Midwest, and Elmore inherited it from his father, Malcolm. Elmore was seventy-seven years old and looked eighty-seven. Lisa was his reward for surviving so long and being worth $1.7 billion. She had everything she wanted, except love.

Elmore was known to drink a bit and forget that he was married. There were days when he wouldn't speak to his trophy wife, but in his defense, an argument could be made that Lisa had very little to say that would have been of interest to Mr. Rathbone. Periodically, when Elmore was bored, according to Lisa, he would require her to dance, to remove her clothes, and then dance some more; he liked to film it. Normally he would then pass out before even taking his Viagra. It usually didn't work anyway, which led to the reason Mrs. Rathbone needed pastoral counseling.

A few weeks ago her old high school boyfriend dropped by to say hello. He was married but had heard Lisa lived in the gated community where he worked as a pool cleaner. They both grew up in trailers in a region just south of Castleton called Ravenswood. He knew her in the biblical sense, and those were good and passionate days of delight and dissipation. He was young, tan, and not given to wearing a shirt that much.

When he knocked on the door and the butler called Lisa, she was so excited she invited him into the house for a glass of tea. He left three hours later after one hour each of slippery sex on the kitchen, dining room, and bedroom floors. It was witnessed by at least three of the staff, and it got back to Elmore.

Lisa's claim that she was just a piece of meat meant she was not appreciated, but she'd played the role very well since the first time she waited on Elmore's table at an Indiana University fund-raiser held at the Marriott Hotel. She practiced what the late Senator Ted Kennedy called Natural Law: "Whatever part of the waitress's body hangs over the table is yours." Elmore patted her on the fanny and then squeezed.

"Very lowbrow," Lisa said.

"Thank you, a little lower please."

They were in love. He loved what he could feel; she loved his bank account. She was reaping what she had sown. She didn't like it, but Michael told her anyway.

Michael listened to her story; she cried. Careful not to console her by touching, he kept his distance. Now Elmore wanted to divorce her and give her nothing; she had signed a prenuptial agreement. She had agreed to a one-time payment of $500,000. She was sure that after taxes she would be unable to maintain her lavish lifestyle. She wanted Michael to help. He knew powerful people, but most important, he knew Elmore, and Elmore would listen.

Mr. Rathbone had given $5 million to the church for the now famous Art Prayer Gardens that brought in many tourists to the church's property and to the church's worship services. Elmore did this because he was very worried, when he was sober, about his eternal home. He didn't attend as much as he used to, but still a couple of times a month he would show up in one of the services.

"Surely, Pastor Michael," Lisa pleaded, "you could help me with this. I would do anything for you if you would help me." Lisa adjusted her skirt just enough to give Michael a look.

"I will pray with the two of you if both of you want to work it out." That was his best offer.

"Our time is up, Lisa. I am recommending you see Dr. Joseph Tucker. He is a friend of mine, and he specializes in your kind of case.

Lisa pouted. "I want to meet with you, Pastor. You make me feel wanted, cared for. I am so relaxed around you."

"I'm sorry, I just can't do that." Michael's tone was meant to assure Mrs. Rathbone that the conversation was over.

"All right." Lisa's voice indicated she was recovering from the rejection. "Can I call you in case of emergency? I may need you to make a house call." She smiled and began to unwind off the couch and wiggle through the door in a way that caught Millie's ire.

When she was gone, Michael smiled at Millie and said, "Whew, that was close." He had survived another test.

Michael plopped a couple of commentaries and his laptop into the front seat of his car and headed off to his study cabin. An elderly couple in the church had deeded it to the church for such uses as retreats and study. For several years now, it was his habit to leave the office at noon on Wednesday and drive north of Noblesville to a three-room cabin only forty minutes away with an idyllic stream bubbling by the back patio. The three rooms were an open area with fireplace, a small kitchen with table, and a bedroom with bath. It was so small it could only accommodate two for any kind of stay.

He would take only water and coffee. He would fast, pray, read, and pretty much write his sermon before he returned home for dinner on Thursday evening. There was no Internet service because it was located nowhere important, a forgettable shack in a nondescript location. It was surrounded by harvested cornfields, like nature's ruins, rough, uneven, not a good place to walk. Central Indiana was flat, with nothing to see except more fields and a few silos, nothing to hear but a few idle chirps, squawks, and moos. It was the closest thing in Michael's life to monasticism. He wondered if this was what Bonhoeffer meant, that any renewal of the church would begin with a new monasticism, nothing like the old.

It was hard to imagine that anything significant could begin in a place devoid of excitement or energy. But it was in this place that Michael seemed to hear that "inner voice" that some people called God. It did occur to him that if God needed this much quiet to speak, not many would be hearing Him.

As he stepped from the car into the silence, it struck him again how he hated being here, he loved being here—he felt good that he was disciplined enough to show up but driven enough that he had to fight off the other voice, "You idiot, what are you doing out here wasting your time?"

He turned off his phone and picked up the Bible; almost every time when God spoke to him, it was when he was reading the Book. The silence was ringing in his ears. If needed, his getaway car was just outside.

— 7 —

By the time Jesús and Antonio pulled themselves out of bed and had lunch, it was 1:30. They were disappointed that all their inquiries regarding the location of Tom Clarke had come up empty. Even Lieutenant Kenny Bohannon had no clue. He could do only so much for them without being noticed. Wherever Clarke was, he wasn't using his car in Marion County or any nearby counties.

Jesús wondered if they should check on Michael Hart. "Shit, let's go by the church."

Antonio turned the car north on Keystone, and they headed to 465. He was the first to admit, "He's not here." They cruised by the house a few minutes later.

"Where the hell is he?" shouted an increasingly agitated Jesús. It was clear that neither knew much about the life of a clergyman, that he might have something to do other than drive between his church and home.

The basic mode for pressuring "clients" was to visit, warn, and administer limited harm. In case of disappearance, flush them out through friends, threaten friends, hurt friends, and squeeze them until the "client" emerged and paid. If they didn't pay, kill. Rarely did they get to the kill option; it had been done, but only with Alonzo's personal go-ahead. Neither Jesús nor Alonzo had ever gotten past limited harm, breaking a bone or two. They always got their money. This was new territory: he was a pastor after all, almost as important as a priest, and there was something different about him.

Antonio turned the Escalade toward the adjacent school building. They decided to wait until school let out so they could get some pictures of Michael Hart's kids. Corey jumped on the bus with Jerry Bohannon. They sat together and talked as the bus made its way onto 82nd Street toward their homes. Jesús took out his Canon SLR with its powerful lens and snapped a few shots of Corey getting off the bus a block from his home.

"This will make them nervous, eh?" Jesús' voice indicated he thought this would flush out Clarke.

*　　*　　*

Tom Clarke loved Naples, especially this time of year on Florida's southwest coast when it cooled down and stopped raining every afternoon. He particularly was enjoying the renewed relationship with his Navy comrade in arms, Joey Ludwig. Joey was one of the most productive snipers in the history of Naval operations. Some called them SEALs, others Special Operations; some were so secret, they had no name. That was Joey; he was still a secret. There would be no books written about his work. The SEALs had an honor code, played by certain rules. Joey had no rules, except survive.

Clarke had run a few missions with Joey, and Joey had spent many a night on the precipice between life and death with Michael Hart. Like many former operators, Joey had made a reputation in the right circles, which meant post-service he had acquired a small fortune selling his skills to the highest bidder. This made life very nice for him in retirement at forty-five. It provided him with Cheryl, twenty-five, and a mini-mansion on the beach.

It was 6:30, and the sun was beginning to set. Two more weeks and standard time would bring a too-early sunset. Cheryl had just left the patio to change out of whatever that was on her body. She might as well have been nude; only a couple of things were covered, but she gave the impression to Clarke that he could see the rest if he wanted.

After his second gin and tonic, he finally asked, "Joey, why do you let her lay around like that? She's got a body that would give Hugh Hefner a stroke."

Joey laughed. "That woman loves me, and you can see how short and ugly I am. She can do what she wants."

Clarke laughed and asked, "Anything?"

"Anything but screw you or anyone else. I'd have to kill them all."

Clarke smiled, not knowing if he meant it or not. Joey got up for another Bud Light. From the back, with his bald head and heavily tattooed thick neck and shoulders, he moved like a tiny human tank as he waddled to the cooler. He had a big smile, he was fun, he was warm, he was deadly.

"Okay, Tom," he said as he came back over. "Why are you here? We love having you around, but you don't just drop in without a reason. What is going down?" Joey waited and took a draw off his fresh cigar.

Clarke sighed. "I got in some trouble up in Indy with some creative bankers—"

"Shit," Joey interrupted. "No, you didn't borrow money from the mob, did you?" Joey was beside himself. "You mean you were gambling again, drinking again of course, and now you're using my place as a safe house?

"Clarke, how many times have we gone over this? You can't keep running back to the boys. You expose us, you pull us back in, and we are retired, we have wives. No one knows where we live, and no one is after us; we've been forgotten. The unforgivable sin is to remind people that we once existed."

Joey dropped into his chair and turned his head toward Clarke in resignation. "Who knows, and where are they?"

Clarke stood and walked to the sand, where he stood looking out to sea. "A couple of thick heads have been following me. They attacked Michael and me outside a Reds game. Michael tuned them up, and now they're following him around."

"Unbelievable." Joey stood up, shaking his head. "You've got the one really righteous guy from our clan involved. He's got a church, a family—Christ, Tommy, you've really...."

Joey's voice trailed off as he walked away cursing Clarke.

✳ ✳ ✳

Clarke knew he was a screwup; he had always depended on his good looks. Some slightly tipsy women had told him he reminded them of James Bond. "Which one?" became his favorite party game as he had gotten older and usually drunker.

The original compliment was issued by a seventeen-year-old admiral's daughter he met right after he had passed BUD/S. Basic Underwater Demolition/SEAL training was something every SEAL had to pass to become a SEAL, but only 10 percent passed. He was feeling pretty good that night. She said Sean Connery, but unlike Connery, Clarke had a beautiful full head of black hair for her to run her barely conscious hands through.

Alcohol is very useful if you want to avoid reality for a while, and who doesn't? How do you abuse two wives, spawn a couple of kids you barely know, and put your old friends in danger? You keep believing you're James Bond. The problem is you are drunk in a sober world. You ignore the words of your once disciple, now mentor/savior/protector and soon-to-be victim, Michael Hart: "God is not mocked, for whatever a man sows, that will he also reap."

✳ ✳ ✳

Joey, Clarke, and Cheryl went out to dinner at the country club where Joey liked to play golf. Clarke borrowed a dinner jacket the restaurant provided. The menus had no prices; if you had to ask, you shouldn't be there.

✳   ✳   ✳

Michael would barely make it for dinner at 6:30. He was doing 85, blowing by almost everything on the road. It had taken him longer than usual to finish his sermon, his concentration had been off. Distraction was not normally a battle, but now it was. He wondered why he hadn't heard from Clarke, constantly was checking his mirrors for cops and for the white Escalade. He took the 82nd Street exit and scooted through his neighborhood. He stopped at the gatehouse and, as usual, Jack the night guard was just getting there. No one would be there midnight. He waved, and Jack waved back, a minute later he was in the garage.

Jen seemed subdued during dinner, nothing anyone except a husband would notice. Corey and Janie chirped about the day, homework, friends, very normal all around.

By nine, the kids were tucked in, and Jen said, "We need to talk." She pulled out an envelope and laid it on the kitchen table. "This was placed on my windshield today while I was at Nordstrom. What does it mean, Michael? I'm scared." Her voice cracked.

Michael opened the manila mailer and pulled out two photographs, one of Corey getting on the bus and a second of Jen herself looking at dresses inside Nordstrom at Keystone Crossing. The pictures were taken with a telephoto lens. It was creepy, but what caused a chill to shoot through Michael's body were the words written in red across both pictures: IS IT SAFE? The infamous words uttered in *The Marathon Man* by Laurence Olivier as he prepared to shove a dental instrument into Dustin Hoffman's gums.

"Who are these people, Michael? Why would anyone want to hurt us? I don't understand."

Michael pulled Jen close as she sobbed. Michael's voice went cold as he softly said, "It will be all right. I will handle it." These thugs had crossed the line. He would notify the police. He knew Jerry's dad was Lieutenant Bohannon in the sheriff's department; he would go directly to him,

"I will try to handle it through proper channels, we can get these guys off our backs." He also wondered, *Where is Tommy Boy? Got to track him down.*

❋　❋　❋

Kenny Bohannon's cell phone vibrated; it was his ex-wife. The lieutenant waited a moment and then picked up. "Yeah." He wanted to keep it brief.

"I gave Michael Hart your cell number; hope you don't mind." Jerry and Hart's boy Corey were good friends."

Sally was in a hurry herself. Bohannon feigned ignorance, wondering out loud, "Why did he want my number?"

Sally answered, "Oh, he said something about a legal question for you. I think he might want to invite you out to coffee; you do need God."

Bohannon twirled in his chair. "All right, see you later."

A few minutes later his phone buzzed again. "Blocked" appeared on the screen. The good lieutenant took a deep breath and accepted the call. "Lieutenant Bohannon, this is Michael Hart. Our sons are friends. Could I have a minute of your time?" The man sounded positive and businesslike.

"Sure, I know of you. Everybody knows who you are, Pastor." Bohannon was diplomatic. "What's on your mind?"

"I have a problem. I'm not sure why I have it, but I would like to meet with you and show you something." The line went quiet.

"Sure, when do you want to do it?" Bohannon's mind was racing. He was sure it had something to do with Jesús, but how would Michael Hart know to call him? It must be a weird coincidence.

"Now." Michael's voice was firm.

"All right, do you want me to come to the church?" Bohannon was almost out of his chair and on his way,

"No"—Michael was emphatic—"Starbucks at Keystone Crossing.

✳ ✳ ✳

Twenty minutes later, Kenny Bohannon and Michael Hart met face to face for the first time. The good lieutenant looked gaunt. His J. C. Penney suit was crawling all over his Barney Fife body. He seemed a bit too nervous, to Michael, for a cop doing a favor.

Michael, as usual, had dressed like the winner he was, in Ralph Lauren khakis, white Façonnable shirt, and new Hugo Boss tweed sports coat. "Thanks for meeting me." With that, Michael pushed the sealed envelope toward Bohannon, who opened the pictures and spent a minute staring at them.

He took a sip of coffee. "What do you think this is, Michael?" Bohannon was playing it as coy as his racing heart would permit.

Michael was leaning forward; he didn't seem like a pastor to Bohannon now. "I think it's a message from the two creeps that have been following me. I want to know something about them. I want the police to get them off my back."

"I can check into it, but I can't really tell you about them. That would be invasion of privacy." Bohannon didn't even sound convincing to himself.

Michael glared at him. "Listen, these guys are invading my privacy, they are threatening my family. Just tell me who they are. Give me an address, some way I can make them go away."

"Sorry, Pastor, I can't do it. I can have someone watch your house, provide some protection for your kids now and then." Bohannon held his ground.

"Listen, Lieutenant," Michael said as he took back the pictures, "you've got to help me. These jerks might even hurt your boy when he's with my boy." Bohannon's insides were churning. He knew of Michael's secret military history. He knew how badly he'd been able to hurt both Jesús and Antonio in that Cincinnati parking lot. He also knew that if he gave up Jesús, he would answer to Alonzo. He feared Alonzo more than Michael.

Suddenly all he wanted was to leave. "Pastor, if it happens again, let me know. We will be looking for these men to question them about your case. As soon as I get back, I'll open a file on them."

The two men stood and walked toward their cars in the mall lot. Michael, fuming, waited until they were nearly at the exit and grabbed Bohannon by the collar. He pulled him into a deserted hallway. Bohannon was up against a wall before he had time to react.

Michael's right hand pinned the lieutenant's neck to the wall. "I want their names, and I want them now."

Bohannon couldn't speak, he couldn't breathe, he started to black out. Michael slammed him to the floor and put his knee into Bohannon's chest, "Who are they? Names, addresses, today."

Michael knew Bohannon was dirty; he just knew it in his bones.

"You can't do this to me." Bohannon choked the words out. "Okay, I'll have the names later today." Michael had taken a chance. If this was an honest cop, he was in trouble. But a dirty cop finally breaks, because he knows you know he would be in even greater trouble.

The lieutenant got back on his feet. "I will let this go. I'll get you the names, but you never got them from me."

Bohannon rushed off to his car. Michael was shaking, not believing he had just done that. Two hours later, he received a text message. It simply said: "Jesus Alvarez 4929 Kingsley Drive 317-400-6221"

He called the number. His well-trained intuition told him direct contact would be best. He knew that the official policy of the US government was not to negotiate with terrorists. Michael was not the government, and Jesús was no terrorist; he was a bumbling fool, but fools can be dangerous. He did, however, park a few doors down from 4929 Kingsley Drive. He might learn something if they were home.

Jesús saw "Blocked" appear on his cell screen, all pastors of large churches have private blocked numbers.

Jesús pressed "Answer." "Hello, who is this?"

Michael drew a breath. "Jesús, this is your new friend, Pastor Michael Hart. We met recently at a baseball game. I was a bit rude; sorry."

Stunned, Jesús' brain went into overdrive, a rare event. "Yeah, why you call me, Padre?"

Michael wanted to play it light. "I noticed you in church the other day. I like to provide pastoral care to new members in their search for truth. In fact, Jesús—and I do like your name—I've seen a lot of you recently, mostly in my rearview mirror. I think I know the answer to the question, but why are you following me, cruising through my neighborhood and taking pictures of my family?"

"Two reasons, Padre," Jesús said, getting into it. "Your

friend Clarke owes me over sixty large. We don't know where he is, but we think you do. And you hurt me and my partner. We don't forget that; you hurt us, and you'll get hurt, real bad, read bad."

Michael felt the adrenaline surge, the anger rising. "Watch your language, Jesús. Don't you realize who you're talking to here?" Michael laughed, knowing he was a good actor. "I'll make a deal with you. I will get Clarke to talk to you, but you must promise to leave my family alone. I'll make you another promise, and I hope you will take this with the utmost seriousness. If you don't leave me, my family, and my church alone, the wrath of God will pour down upon you."

Jesús stood up, turned and twisted his body around the floor as though he was dancing. "Hey, man, you must have powerful prayers. You are the one who is going to need to pray. Get Clarke to us in the next twenty-four hours, or something bad will happen to your pretty little kids."

Michael sat quiet for moment and then said, "Jesús, I will get Clarke here. May God have mercy on your soul." He threw his phone across the car.

Jesús pressed end call. He didn't know if Michael's words were the prayer of a pastor or the promise of an assassin.

Immediately Michael called Clarke's mobile. Tommy Boy recognized the number but didn't want to answer. Cheryl's well-oiled body was slithering on top of his. Joey was at the driving range. One hour alone with Joey's girl was all "Bond, James Bond" needed. It always amazed humankind how little time it took for fools to repeat their folly.

He picked up anyway. "Michael, how are you? What's up?" Cheryl did the obligatory giggle when interrupted in the midst of her virtuosic performance.

Michael was steamed. "Listen, Tommy Boy, get your

butt over to my house from wherever you are. I just talked with your banker, and he has been following my family."

Clarke was startled. "Whoa, Michael, I'm in Florida. It will take me a few days to get back up there."

"You've got twenty-four hours; take a plane." Michael hung up.

Just then Clarke heard the garage door opening. Joey was back. Cheryl ran to the shower, and Tommy Boy buttoned things up, pretending he was playing a game on his phone. "Hey, Joey, did you hit 'em straight?" he asked in an offhand manner.

Joey ignored the question. "Where's Cheryl?"

"She's in your bedroom, I think; don't really know." To Joey, Clarke was a bit too blasé. He didn't naturally trust anyone, especially Clarke—actually, not even Cheryl.

Clarke was trying to figure out how to bring up the subject. "Joey, I've got to go. I just got a call from Michael, and he needs me in Indy in the next twenty-four hours."

Joey raised an eyebrow. "I don't suppose it's to sing in the choir tomorrow night." It was clear he wanted to know more.

"No, we have to deal with my problem with the Mexican Mafia bankers, something urgent. I'm going to book a flight for first thing in the morning."

Joey suddenly felt a rush of relief, knowing Clarke was leaving. "You let me know if you guys need any help, but only if it's an emergency. Make sure Michael knows that I offered." With that, Joey walked toward the bedroom and Clarke punched in the American Airlines number on his phone.

— 8 —

Friday was the day for cleaning up details in preparation for Saturday night and Sunday services. The weekend would bring more than 10,000 men, women, boys, and girls through the doors of The Challenge church. Various worship teams had to time out their sets, and the sermon had to calibrated for television.

Michael spent the morning in meetings with his media teams and worship and arts staff. He didn't lunch with anyone on Friday. The hours of 12:00–2:00 were sacrosanct; he would edit and polish his message. At 2:00 PM on Friday, the sermon was ready.

He then had until 5:00 PM Saturday night to get his soul ready. Truth poured through personality. He would preach to the confused, troubled, arrogant, biased, angry, hurting, and hypocritical saints who were seeking for comfort, assurance, answers, and some direction in this world split apart between good and evil. But this weekend would be different. Somehow, by Sunday evening, there needed to be some resolution with the two men who threatened Michael's way of life.

Early Saturday morning, Clarke was aboard American flight 481 from Miami to Indianapolis, landing at 11:00 AM. Michael and Jen slipped out to a favorite breakfast joint while Corey and Janie got ninety minutes of absolute freedom to watch TV or play video games. Date night had gone kaput a bit because neither Jen nor Michael could free their minds. Michael was not willing to answer Jen's questions, and she grew angry. He had decided overnight that this morning he would tell her a bit more.

"Listen Jen, I am going to tell you why these men sent the pictures." Michael had feared this moment. For years he had told Jen nearly nothing about his military experience. Usually he got away with bare bones: that he was in Naval Intelligence, but that nothing very important happened from 1994 to 1999. Pretty routine, sitting in a white van in Kiev listening to how Sasha and Anatoly, a couple of former KGB spies, spent their weekend. Jen thought her very smart husband spent five years analyzing data. Still, he was not prepared to say much.

"Jen, I've thought it over. I need to come clean with you about what has happened." Jen already was softening,

"You know all about Tom Clarke and me—how he led me to Christ at Butler, how he discipled me for two years, and how we both went into Naval Intelligence after graduation, right?"

Jen said, "Of course. What does that have to do with this?"

He took a deep breath. "Tom was in Special Operations, a Navy SEAL. He was and is a brilliant man. He can remember almost anything and everything. He had a great career and would still be a high-ranking officer if not for three things: women, booze, and gambling—not necessarily in that order, but it doesn't matter: he made too many mistakes."

She was getting the picture. "Which one in this case?"

He smiled. "Well, all of the above, but the problem is he borrowed fifty thousand dollars from some loan sharks. He hasn't been able to repay, they know I am his friend, they can't find him, so they are harassing me."

Jen looked puzzled. "Yeah, but why threaten a pastor and his family? Wouldn't that make headlines?"

Michael allowed himself a sheepish grin. "There is a bit more to the story. They followed us to Cincinnati, to the Reds game a few weeks ago, and they jumped us in the parking lot. As you know, sweetie, I'm forty, but I haven't forgotten what I learned about self-defense in the military.

I just got mad, the adrenaline shot through my veins, and Tom and I beat the crap out of them. They kind of took it personally, so they may want to return the favor as a matter of principle. These guys operate on fear: if you don't fear them, they've got nothing, they are out of business." Michael leaned back, expecting the worst from Jen.

She laughed, and her face turned red. She seemed embarrassed that the chance of her family being hurt struck her as funny. "My beautiful pastoral baby," she said, struggling to get the words out, "you've gone and got yourself in a little boys' game. Sounds like a pissing contest, who's got the biggest you know what." She collapsed on to her side, "Sorry, honey, it all just hit my funny bone. What are you going to do, 'rub them out'?" And she started laughing again.

Michael was stunned. Little Jenny from Elkhart thinks the Mexican Mafia is funny. He grabbed her by the hand. "Jen, this is serious! I don't know what they are going to do, but Clarke is returning today. After church tomorrow, I am going to meet with these guys and see if we can work something out. I suppose you could say that we are in negotiations. Clarke doesn't have very much money. I am thinking we can talk them into some alternative, but these guys normally don't allow you to make payments."

Suddenly Jen got concerned about the kids and stood up. "Let's go, Michael." They returned home to find both Corey and Janie happy and safe. Michael had opened the door to his past, and it was a dark and graceless world. He didn't want to go back there, and he certainly didn't want to take Jen and the kids there. He was committed to keeping them safe. They would never need to know what took place in the bowels of the earth.

✻ ✻ ✻

Clarke touched down at Indianapolis International at 11:13 and went directly to the car service, scanning the large new terminal for his two Hispanic friends. He greeted the driver with the name plate, "Arnold Toynbee." Being a history buff, he liked using a historian's alias. Thirty minutes later he was in Michael's living room.

Jen was busying herself with Janie and only poked her head in the room to say, "Hi, Tommy, hope you will stay for dinner."

Clarke simply smiled. "Probably not, Jen. You know it will be a busy twenty-four hours."

Michael came in and said, "Let's go downstairs into my study."

They descended into a world-class man cave; the brick walls were lined with framed pictures of the Big Red Machine. There they were, Murderer's Row: Pete Rose, Joe Morgan, Johnny Bench, Tony Perez, Davy Concepción, George Foster, César Gerónimo, the only team to win seven games with no losses on the way to the World Series championship in 1976. The rest of the room was devoted to Indiana basketball memorabilia: signed pictures from Tom and Dick VanArsdale, Jimmy Rayl, Bobby Knight, Gene Keady, and even John Wooden when he was coach at South Bend Central.

At the center of the back wall was Michael's tribute to the greatest Purdue basketball player of all time, Terry Dischinger, a three-time first team All-American and member of the first dream team, the 1960 Rome Olympics basketball team with Jerry West and Oscar Robertson. Dischinger set a record that still stands for double-doubles, double-digit points, and rebounds. He did it fifty times in three years, remarkably.

There were telltale signs of Michael's past, the Navy Cross framed and hung over the fireplace. He always joked that it was for being the bravest sailor by dating the admiral's homely daughter in his first year.

They took a seat on his beautiful leather chairs meant for long hours of sports viewing on the 55-inch high-def flat screen. The action was so real you would actually jump out of the way sometimes.

Michael grabbed the remote and turned on SportsCenter to drown out any discussion. "I've got a meeting set up tonight at 6:30 at the Broad Ripple Wings place. That's where they met you, right?"

Michael was whispering, but Clarke understood. "And what the hell am I going to do? I only have twelve thousand dollars of their money!" Clarke muffled his voice but not his concern. "They don't do lines of credit like a bank."

"That's all right." Michael preened a bit. "We'll make a deal. They can't afford to go home empty-handed. So tonight, 6:30, Broad Ripple Wings."

It was a Sunday like many others: five services, shaking hands, listening to the comments from inanities like "a sermon for the ages" to "Pastor, I would prefer more uplifting messages. We don't need to hear so much about the negative within ourselves."

This had been and continued to be the ying and the yang of teaching the same people over and over. It was what made a man tired, feeling so weary that only a laydown would do. But Michael had to keep it going. Maybe the most crucial message of his day was yet to be delivered.

He met Clarke a block from Broad Ripple Wings, the home of Buffalo Wild Wings, a yellow and black building. It was easy to find and noisy, a prerequisite for such a discussion. It was open and loud: everyone could hear your voice, but no one could understand you unless you were whispering in their ear. It had the needed anonymity and the intimacy; no one could record it because of background noise. The two slipped into the bar and took two seats at a table with plenty of room for at least two more.

Jesús and Antonio saw them enter Buffalo Wild Wings. Antonio said, "If he doesn't have the money tonight, ask for a payment. Give him another week." His motive was to keep Jesús alive, avoid more trouble, and start getting the money back.

"Hell no. They give it all tonight, or we hurt the kid."

Antonio protested, "You need to talk to Alonzo. That's kidnapping; even AA can't get you out of that." Antonio shook his head and turned the engine on.

Jesús grabbed the wheel. "We're going in."

Antonio turned off the car and got out. Inside, they spotted Michael and Clarke and headed to their table.

Michael stood, pointed to the chairs, and said, "Have a seat, gentlemen. What would you like to drink?"

Jesús smiled. "I'll take a Mexican whore." He threw his head back with laughter. "The drink, not the woman. Mix some amaretto and tequila, and shake real good."

Antonio said, "Budweiser."

Jesús looked at Clarke. "Where you been, Cacos? You've been stealing from me. Where is the money?"

Clarke looked at him for a moment. "I've only got twelve thousand right now. I know where I can get the rest, but it could take a couple of weeks."

Jesús smiled and checked the surrounding tables. "Listen, Tommy, you have disrespected me. You hide, you run, you lie, how can I do business with you? I can't trust you, you're unreliable."

Jesús was quite proud of himself. He loved talking down to the white man.

"You can't have a week, or three days. You get twenty-four more hours, and we are going to find you, and we will end this business."

Michael leaned in to Jesús. Antonio reached slowly for his gun. "Look, boys, last time we tangled, we tuned you up pretty good. I know you didn't like the pain and the rehab. You will let Tommy figure out how to pay in a reasonable time frame; otherwise you guys might spend a bit more time in the hospital than you would like."

Jesús laughed again. "Come on, Padre, just because you got the jump on us, that doesn't mean it can happen again. Me and my homies will be ready, and we will put you all in the nearest sewer."

Then he nodded. "I'll tell you what, Preacher. Reach out to all those suckers who give you money on TV."

And with that, Jesús and Antonio made their exit, confident that Clarke and the preacher would back down and find money, and it would be over.

*   *   *

Two days later, with no news or money from Clarke, Jesús and Antonio were looking intently through field glasses, seeing exactly how long it took for Corey Hart to walk home from the bus. The stop on 92nd Street was where Corey and Jerry Bohannon got off the bus together to walk to their homes in the Hamptons at Geist. Not usually where preachers and police lieutenants bought homes. It was, however, where megachurch pastors and police lieutenants with supplemented incomes did live.

After Jerry's house, Corey would have another mile to go before reaching his gate. By now they knew that Jerry Bohannon was Corey's friend, the son of the cop who'd sold them out to Michael Hart. Why not put a bit of a scare into him as well?

"Let's give them both a free night's lodging at the Holiday Inn Express." At that point, they reasoned, the crooked cop, Clarke, and Michael Hart would come up with the money.

* * *

Michael told Clarke, "Wait them out; they are flunkies. They won't do anything without the okay from on high. I think our best bet is to convince them to move on, write it off as a bad debt, or take a partial payment. They aren't desperate yet; if I'm wrong and they bring in reinforcements, we will need some ourselves."

Clarke's phone rang; it was Jesús. "Got it yet? I hope you do; don't want to see anyone hurt." He sounded like a caring insurance broker.

"Not yet," Clarke replied. "I've got a couple of real promising deals about to close. I'll be able to pay you this month."

Without another word, Jesús ended the call. He and Antonio were the type of men who would commit to war without knowing their enemy. They gave fresh meaning to "fools rush in where angels fear to tread." They had no permission from Alonzo and no knowledge of who might pay the ransom, but they decided to take Corey and Jerry because they would not be disrespected.

They had seen it work many times before. Alonzo would order his men to take a family member, and after a few hours, the family sold their business or otherwise came up with the cash, the building permit, whatever it was. It worked 95 percent of the time. They knew that Michael and Clarke could create some trouble, but they didn't have a worldwide terror squad at their disposal as Jesús and Antonio did.

* * *

It was another school day. Tuesday was about as normal as any day could get. Michael started by snuggling up next to Jen's lovely bare bottom for some comforting contact before having to hop out of bed. There was only one problem. The longer he stayed in contact, the more he wanted to stay.

As his interest grew, Jen finally noticed and grabbed his growing enthusiasm, gave it a friendly squeeze, and hopped out of bed herself. "Sorry, Captain Kirk, can't beam you up this morning. Got to get breakfast going."

Captain Kirk was left with nothing to do but get dressed for a day on this planet. It had been the pattern to drive the kids in the morning, but Corey liked to ride the bus with Jerry, so they let him.

Michael was convinced that no one would seriously go after his boy. He had warned them, and they were not that crazy. *After all, my son is my son, he is protected, we prayed and dedicated him years before that God would put a hedge of protection around him.*

Michael waved good-bye to Corey as he headed off to the bus. He turned back to his bowl of Wheaties with bananas and of course the obligatory yogurt. He couldn't help but ask, "Whatever happened to biscuits and gravy? We've forgotten how to eat good food."

Jen wanted to go in with him today. The artistic community luncheon would be at 12:30, and she had a lot to do to get ready to greet the 450 women who would be in attendance. The special speaker would be Dr. Susan Hollis, director of the Indianapolis Museum of Art. As usual there would be a panel discussion afterward on the Christian story as told through the arts. Jen wouldn't be done until Janie got out of school at 3:00.

Michael took Mondays off, so this was his first day back in the office. First things first, a meeting with Millie. "Some members of the Leadership Community want some time; apparently they are unhappy that you are requiring every group leader to stay in an accountable relationship."

Millie smiled as she handed Michael the schedule.

"Nothing new there, Millie." Michael didn't even look up. "Give them 3:00 PM on Thursday." He sighed. "I keep having problems with Joe Franklin's area. He is a small group guru, but he's a relational disaster. How does that happen?"

Millie looked at him over the top of her readers. "I told you there was something not right with him, but you had your mind made up."

Michael laughed. "You're always right, Millie. Why don't I listen to you?"

She smiled. "That is a mystery, isn't it, sir?"

Millie was five-one and weighed too much for her delicate frame. She didn't walk; instead, she rotated her hips, and somehow her feet caught up just in time to keep her upright. Her readers were perched on the tip of her nose; nothing got by her. If you wanted any of Michael's time or to get on his good side, you would need to please Millie first. She was schoolmarm, sergeant-at-arms, executive assistant, and mother confessor in one. She protected Michael from sales personnel, ministry promoters, and mostly, his own staff of more than sixty full-time pastors and assistants and part-time interns, not including the grade 1–8 teachers and administrators.

Michael's office was a fortress, and Millie stood guard along with Jacque Ellie, the church's full-time security guard. Michael asked Jacque to tell him if he saw anyone on church property who looked suspicious. He'd told Michael about the white Cadillac Escalade that had cruised through the parking a lot a couple of times recently. The windows were smoked, so he couldn't give a description of the driver or his passenger, but Michael didn't need one.

Michael was having trouble with focus. He kept mulling over his next move. What would these two dunderheads do? How dangerous were they really? It was only six weeks to his Annual Leadership Challenge. Twenty-five hundred pastors and church leaders would descend on The Challenge's campus for a three-day look-see at "success." This thirsty throng of mostly pastors would gather around the trough of programs, ideas, and big portions of inspiration. They took home a bagful of books, program guides, DVDs, and ideas. Unfortunately, they couldn't take home Michael, and they had to take themselves home.

Michael's church represented less than 0.5 percent of all churches in America. It was odd even to Michael why so many would dedicate themselves to try and duplicate what few of them could do. This was not God's plan for them, he told them every year, but they just kept coming back for more. Michael's goal was to teach them about what God wanted from them and what every one of them could succeed at: to be disciples and to make disciples.

He knew if it wasn't for the church's numbers, no one would be interested. He normally started his keynote message every year with the statement, "Nothing fails like success." But right now, he was worried about his family, his friend Tommy Boy, and how to end this nightmare.

* * *

Jesús kept ignoring Antonio's pleas to call Alonzo. "Listen, man, you've got to get permission from AA. You can't do this; it could start a major shitstorm."

Jesús grabbed the steering wheel and pounded it with both hands. "Shut up. I'll worry about Alonzo. Your job is to help me, *comprendes?*"

Antonio couldn't believe they were there, fifty yards from the bus stop, where in five minutes Corey Hart and Jerry Bohannon would exit their bus to walk home.

Soon the yellow bus with THE CHALLENGE ACAD-

EMY on the side pulled to a stop, and the boys got off. Jesús edged the SUV slowly toward the boys as the bus disappeared around the corner. Both boys carried their school bags over their shoulders, unsuspectingly climbing the hilly street away from their looming captors. They both wore the blue and white colors required for the school uniform, their jackets slung over their shoulders.

Jesús accelerated to beyond the boys and blocked their path, Antonio opened the door and flashed a .357 Magnum revolver. He grabbed Corey and told Jerry to get in the car. The boys were frozen in fear; it took them ten seconds in all. Jesús closed the SUV door and rolled out of the neighborhood with due speed.

When Corey finally was able to speak, he asked, "What is this—what are you doing?"

"Shut up!" Antonio yelled. "Give me your hands." He grabbed Corey's hands and cuffed them with a plastic cord.

Jerry was crying, but he managed to say, "You are going to be sorry. My dad is a cop."

Jesús turned, cursing beneath his breath. "You heard the man. Put your hands behind your back." Antonio jammed hoods over the boys' heads and ordered them to lie down.

They had rented an old mechanic's garage just off 38th and Keystone. Fifteen minutes later, they were tucked away in it, door down. It was time to make the call.

Jesús was elated. "This will teach these choirboys to mess with us. Now I will call them, then I will call Alonzo."

Antonio looked troubled. "Jesús, did you hear what that one kid said? That his dad is a cop?"

Jesús looked up in surprise. "Is that what he said?"

"Yeah, Jesús, that is what he said." Antonio gave him that disgusted look when someone realizes they just screwed up.

Jesus walked over to the hooded, sobbing Jerry Bohannon. "Hey, kid, what's your name?" He pulled the hood off the boy's head.

"Jerry Bohannon. My dad is Lieutenant Bohannon." The boy was still shaking.

They walked away, and Antonio had to say it: "Are you sure we want to go through with this?" He gave Jesús an earnest look. "We have just kidnapped the son of the only friend we have in the entire police force in this county."

"Yeah, but we're only going to keep them until they give up Clarke." Jesús was trying to deflect the blame. "I'm going to call Hart now. He'll give us Clarke, and we'll give him his kid back."

* * *

Jen returned home with Janie around 3:30; time for a snack. Janie loved a Swiss cheese quesadilla or a chocolate protein shake. Today she wanted the shake. After a few minutes of monitored TV, there was some homework before dinner. Around 4:30, Jen began to wonder about Corey. She thought she would call Sally Bohannon to see if Jerry and Corey were at their place.

* * *

It was 4:40 when Michael's mobile rang—a blocked number. He didn't want to answer; he was just finishing up a conversation with his senior high pastor who'd caught him in the hallway. "Hey, I have to take this call. See you later." With that, he pushed answer.

"Hey, preacher man, got some news for you."

Michael recognized Jesús' voice and was instantly apprehensive. "Hey, we need more time."

Jesús' voice was cocky. "I just couldn't wait to give you the news. I've got your boy here; he and his buddy are enjoying the pleasure of my company."

An electric shock spiked through Michael's body, and something like a fist grabbed him deep in his stomach. "What are you talking about, Jesús?" He thought it must be a poor attempt at humor.

"What, you didn't hear me? Here, why don't you talk to him?"

Corey yelled into the phone, "Dad, they got us. I don't know what to do."

The sound of Corey's voice startled Michael. Immediately his mind and body locked down into emergency mode. "Don't worry, son, this will be over soon." He kept his voice calm.

"Here's the deal, Preacher." Jesús was feeling his power. "You give up Clarke, and your boy will be home for a late dinner."

Michael's tone changed. "Here's my deal, Jesús. You send those boys home right now, and I won't kill you tonight."

Jesús was flustered but trying to keep up the bravado. "Big talk for a preacher. You come after me and your boy is dead." He wasn't going to back down.

Michael remained firm: "You haven't considered the other boy. His dad is a cop. You have very little time before all hell is going to rain down on you. Jesús, by dawn you will be either dead or in jail, and I'm betting on dead."

He hung up and immediately called Clarke. "You need to meet me at my house in one hour. They have taken Corey and Bohannon's son, Jerry."

Then he called Kenny Bohannon. "The two thugs you are protecting kidnapped our boys off the school bus two hours ago. They have them somewhere in the city. Meet me at my house in one hour."

Bohannon was livid. "Those sons o' bitches, they can't do this. I'm going to send SWAT out there,"

Michael interrupted, "No, no, that is not the play. We need to think this through before we act. My house, one hour."

By the time Michael got home, Jen and Sally were worried about what kind of trouble Corey and Jerry had gotten into. Sally had driven over, looking for them along the way, and was seated at the kitchen table sipping tea. Had they gone home with some boys or, worse, with some girls?

When Michael walked through the door, the look on his face said it all. Janie was sent to her room, and Michael sat down with Jen and Sally. He paused and then said, "I don't know how to explain this, but Corey and Jerry have been taken."

Jen cried out, "No, no, this can't be happening."

Sally was befuddled. "What are you talking about? Taken…what do you mean, taken? By whom, for what?"

He explained, "I don't think they will hurt them. They are trying to scare us."

By now Jen was screaming. "It worked; I'm scared. Michael, you fix this. Why have you let this happen? I don't know you—who are you?" She ran from the room to find Janie.

An hour later, Jen and Sally had calmed down, and Lieutenant Bohannon and Tom Clarke had joined them.

The air was thick around the table. Jen was furious with Tommy and Michael; Sally was demanding her ex-husband call in SWAT, the Indiana National Guard, FBI, CIA, and all of Jerry's superhero action figures.

The problem was that the good lieutenant couldn't call anyone in without exposing his connection to Jesús and Antonio. Michael was not able to talk freely with Jen and Sally present, but they wouldn't leave, demanding to know everything.

Michael said carefully, "Before we call in anyone, is there a simple way to get the boys back that would lower the risk for the kidnappers and the boys?"

"Money," Jen blurted out, "how much money can we beg and borrow, then will they let them go?"

Michael rubbed his chin. "Not bad, Jen. We've got twenty-two thousand saved, and Tommy has twelve. What do you have, Bohannon?"

Sally, in particular, was interested in the answer. "I've got some; I can cover the rest." Sally wanted to ask, but she held back. She wouldn't forget this hidden money that the perpetually broke Kenny Bohannon miraculously seemed to possess now.

Michael scooted his chair forward. "All right. We'll pay them the sixty-two thousand, get the boys back, and then worry about the ramifications later."

Michael bowed his head, and they all joined hands around the table.

"Oh God, maker of heaven and earth, please, we beg you to protect our boys, restrain the wicked hands of these men. May you cause our boys to trust you in this. We pray that you would give them peace and that they would be back in our arms very soon. We claim this in the mighty name of Christ, amen."

When Michael's phone rang again, he, Clarke, and Bohannon were driving home with the $62,000 in hand. Michael couldn't access his funds until the bank opened the next morning, but Bohannon had it all in cash. You don't put Bohannon's kind of money in the bank; you don't want any records.

"We've got the money, Jesús. Where do you want to meet for the exchange?"

Michael was eager. Jesús was surprised but was ready to deal. "Meet us at nine sharp in front of the Marriott Hotel at the Circle downtown. I will pull up beside you, you bring me the money, and then the boys will get in your car. No cops."

Michael was not picky. "Okay, done." Michael felt in his gut that it would be a clean deal, but he still wasn't sure he could go through with it. It was just so galling to pay these losers the money. Just in case he changed his mind, Clarke would be fifty feet away in a separate car with a Barska telescopic rifle trained on Jesús' noggin; any problem, and splat goes the "taco head." That would get Antonio's attention. He would run, and the boys would be free.

Just before 9:00 PM, Michael and Bohannon pulled up to the edge of the passenger drop at the Marriott's front door. It was a rainy Tuesday night, with no Pacer or Colt game; downtown was empty. Michael looked up at the Soldiers' and Sailors' Monument. Not one tourist, not one bum…it could have been 3:00 AM. No one could see that the creative Tom Clarke had parked two blocks away and had stationed himself on the monument behind a statue. He was ready if needed.

The familiar Escalade slipped around the corner and pulled up behind Michael. He took the satchel of money and walked back to Jesús, who was behind the wheel. The window came down, and Michael saw the smile on Jesús' face.

"Hey, Padre, I knew you would see the light."

Michael was stone faced. "Okay, here it is. I'll hand it to you when I see the boys get out of the car." He handed the money to Jesús but kept a good grip. He saw Jerry and Corey in back, and they looked okay. Antonio opened the door, and they hopped out.

Michael let go of the bag. The boys ran to his car and jumped in. Michael happily climbed in behind the wheel; when he looked back, the Escalade was already gone. The boys and their fathers embraced, and then Michael texted Jen, "Got 'em."

✳   ✳   ✳

Jen and Sally embraced, and tears were flowing. Though only a few hours had passed since the kidnapping, it had seemed like an eternity. Thirty minutes later, Corey was having a grilled cheese and tomato soup late night dinner, just as Jesús had predicted.

When Michael pulled Jen in for a hug as they met in the safety of their bed, somehow he knew it wasn't over. Especially once Jesús discovered that just underneath Clarke's $12,000 was nothing but paper and a note from Michael:

Jesús,
I didn't kill you tonight because I want you to go away. That is the reason I told my sniper not to split your melon. If you go away, no harm will come to you and Antonio, but if you harass me or my family in any way, my graciousness toward you will cease.
Have a nice day.

He just couldn't bring himself to let Jesús win; it was his stubbornness. He had honed this quality for many years: don't let the bad guys win, never let them have the upper hand, or they will rule you forever. Michael knew it wasn't over. It never is when there is an equally stubborn kingpin on the other side who hates losing as much as you do.

— 9 —

Jesús felt more stupid than usual after he read the note. It occurred to him—and usually things occurred to Jesús after they had occurred to others—that Michael Hart, Ken Bohannon, and Tom Clarke all knew him and what he had done. He was a bit bumfuzzled, but he needed a strategy to keep them quiet, because kidnapping at one time was punishable by death and still meant a long sentence in federal prison. Most of all, he wanted his money.

He had been fooled again. He couldn't return home or even tell his brother about this. He had to think, which was very hard for Jesús, his weakness, in fact. He put his foot through the drywall of the dining room, threw a vase into the kitchen sink, and finished off his time of meditation with a pint of Jack Daniels. Nothing like thinking things through.

✳   ✳   ✳

Alonzo's phone vibrated on the countertop. His hands were wrapped around a bottle of Staropramen beer, his favorite while in Prague. He loved the best, and his suite at the Hotel Paris was the very best. A neo-Gothic building with art nouveau elements, it had superb doors and golden trim on the ceilings; everything was in pristine condition.

He didn't need to hide anymore; he was feared here more than respected. He was dirty, but no one could prove it. He now lived above the radar. The hotel staff, the police, even the secret police met his needs and left him alone. They knew he could buy them, sell them, or kill them, depending on his mood.

He first fell in love with what was then the Pariz in

the early years of Czech freedom because it had an open restaurant. He would walk there on early mornings from his cheap hotel because he could afford their breakfast but not their rooms. Now he used their three best suites for his entourage.

The screen read, 317-444-7653, Ken Bohannon. Alonzo picked up the phone and pushed answer. "Kenny, my boy, I hope this is a personal call and not about Jesús?"

Kenny cleared his throat. "I love you too, AA." Bohannon followed his attempt at humor with a forced laugh.

Alonzo actually laughed himself. "All right, you haven't called in months. What is it?"

Bohannon was careful. "Jesús and Antonio loaned a local fifty k. He didn't pay on time, and they started the normal collection procedure. They attempted to shake him down in a parking lot, but the guy and his friend beat the crap out of them. The guy's friend is a minister. They met, they talked, but Jesús couldn't take it that he had been bested by a preacher, so he and Antonio decided to kidnap the preacher's son, and my son was with him, so they took them both."

Alonzo couldn't believe what he was hearing and interrupted, "Kenny, this is a joke, right? You're drunk. Put Jesús on the line, the little pimp. I'm not eating this shit sandwich." Alonzo laughed and took another swig of beer.

"I'm serious, AA. We had to come up with the fifty K plus twelve K interest, sixty-two K in all to get our boys back. Two things, AA: I don't like my son being kidnapped, and I'm out thirty K. Well, I suppose I should tell you that I'm not really out the thirty because the pastor only gave Jesús twelve, so Jesus is light by thirty-eight K and all the interest."

Alonzo was silent, his mind racing, his famous anger boiling up inside. "Where are Jesús and Antonio?"

Bohannon replied, "I don't know, haven't seen them

since the exchange, and they haven't called. I'm sure they are worried about what I am going to do."

"Don't worry about your money. I will call my little brother and see what demon has entered his mind."

Keeping a lid on his temper, Alonzo probed. "Can you protect them? The preacher isn't going to file any charges, is he? You can stop that, right?"

Alonzo formed it as a question, but Bohannon took it as an order. "Nah, they don't want anyone to know about it. I worry more about the boys themselves bragging about it at school." Bohannon just thought of this problem as the words came out of his mouth. He covered himself at once: "We've already warned the boys about talking and told them how if any of this gets out, it will hurt their fathers. Neither of us wants any of this to go public."

"What about the guy who owed the money?" Alonzo didn't overlook anything; that was why he was rich, feared, and alive.

"He is beholden to the pastor. They have been lifelong friends; he gets it. You can't predict, however, his future sins. He is known as smart and crazy, crazy for women, booze, and the ponies."

Bohannon hung up the phone only after giving Alonzo two names, Michael Hart and Tom Clarke. He told Alonzo that he didn't see any problem with them. He would watch them, though he didn't know if Alonzo believed that.

*　　*　　*

After Jesús got off the phone with Alonzo, he felt smaller, dumber, and more disgraced than ever before. He had been ordered home to New York City to be just a *travieso* again, a misfit. He was boiling inside; he wanted his revenge. He would take his revenge against the preacher, his family, and Tom Clarke. If he was going to be a failure at home, he would rather be dead, but at least the people who'd made him look so bad and make such poor decisions would be dead too.

Thus ran the twisted thoughts of a man with no moral compass. He had never experienced acceptance; he didn't have an identifiable soul; his instincts were those of a wounded and cornered animal. He was wounded, but he wasn't cornered. All he had to do was leave, but that was not an option for Jesús Alvarez. He wanted the money, but more than that, he wanted revenge.

✳ ✳ ✳

Michael was settling in again to a semi-normal life, trying to push away the inevitable worries that came with his knowledge of treacherous human nature. He and Bohannon had agreed not to press charges, to keep it all quiet. That would be best for their families and their careers. It would not help for the media to learn that Michael had certain skills or that he had made certain deals with kidnappers, and it would not help the good lieutenant's career for them to know he'd cooperated with a kidnapper without even informing his own Marion County Sheriff's Department. He would remain their secret.

The problem for Michael would now be to extricate himself from the old world where trust was rare, treachery common, and cynicism essential. He taught his congregation that the healthiest environment for human flourishing required relationships of trust, grace, acceptance, submission, and affirmation. The key question to another person or group is "Can I trust me with you?"

In Michael's discipleship in Special Operations, that was a question for only a handful of others. Everyone else was roadkill. When Corey and his family were in danger, he dropped almost immediately into that dark place that had made him a man to be feared, a man you wouldn't want to know or be close to. He didn't want that man to come back into his life.

He kept flipping back and forth as he drove to work, praying that he would be able to get back to the happy warrior for Christ who saw theological principles as the bedrock for running the world. But he knew there were some other rules in the world that didn't fit any theological textbook; he believed in them, too. Was his spiritual leadership a fantasy, a Mary Poppins world where Dick Van Dyke and Julie Andrews went flying about with umbrellas, holding tea parties in the air?

For the first time, Michael, Jen, Corey, and Janie had a family secret. They agreed this was the most important secret they could ever have, even more secret than that Daddy sometimes said "shit." Since Corey had been taken after school and was home a few hours later, he didn't miss a beat. The next day everyone was at school; that was the way the Harts liked to handle issues. Michael and Jen did worry about slips of the tongue, particularly from Janie, but she didn't know that much.

Jen and Michael were both athletic. Michael worked out for forty-five minutes, six days a week. He had a gym at home, a section of his three-car garage. He had made a separate room and drywalled it himself. Inside was a treadmill for the winter months, a simple weight-lifting bench, and a rack of free weights.

He had a routine that had worked for him: stretching ten minutes, one hundred push-ups and sit-ups, for ten minutes, running twenty minutes, stretching five minutes. If it was above freezing, he would often run outside and even extend his workout on longer days to running some hills around the housing development.

On the other hand, Jen was all about yoga and running. Both had hard bodies for their late thirties or early forties, and they liked nice clothes and fashion that accentuated their good looks. Jen looked particularly fetching as she ran through the neighborhood with her insulated green tights, snow white Nike Windbreaker, and blond hair up in a ponytail. The pink earmuff ring accented her running shoes. She looked like she was running on air as she glided along.

*   *   *

Antonio snapped another picture. Jesús was licking his lips. "Nice ass; I'm going to have myself some of that." The sound of his voice would have creeped out Madonna.

The plan was simple, strike terror in the heart of the preacher man about his trophy wife. Let him know that at any minute she could be an object of sexual perversion, some very dangerous man's adult toy. They had pics of her shopping, picking up Janie at ballet lessons, sitting in the sun reading the paper at Starbucks, and a few through the windows of the Hart home in various stages of undress.

Jen liked to cool down and stretch on the floor where the warm autumn sun streamed in through the windows, just where a telephoto lens could find its mark. She never removed all her clothes, but she revealed enough to stop any man walking by or to slow an interested motorist. It was only a performance for those peering through the photo lens with malicious intent.

Antonio thought he had enough to do the job. They made their way back to 4929 Kingsley Drive so he could crop and edit with Photoshop. It only took two hours for them to select the photos, write the threats in red across them, and put them in the mail. They would arrive the next afternoon at the Hart home. In the meantime, they would look for Clarke. They had lost a friend in Bohannon, so they would have to do this on their own. Alonzo couldn't know about it. They were reduced to checking local bars.

＊　＊　＊

Tom Clarke would be hard to find. With Michael's help, he had checked himself into the Monastery of the Immaculate Conception, a beautiful castle on a hill in Ferdinand, a hamlet in southern Indiana. The Sisters of St. Benedict ran the place, but they would allow a male visitor who was required to live in solitude in a guesthouse on the edge of the property.

When he checked in, the sister handed Clarke his room key and said, "Let us know if there is anything you think you need, and we'll teach you to live without it." Clarke chuckled, but he knew if he could learn to live without a few things, it would be the key to his life getting better. He could stay as long as he could stand it. Michael told him to stay there until further notice. He gave Clarke a book by Henri Nouwen, *In the Name of Jesus*.

"Tommy," Michael advised, "you need to learn the basic lessons of this book. Read it, think about it, walk around the grounds and pray. Just don't call me or leave here until I come and get you. You need some silence and solitude. It will probably be more difficult than some of your missions, but it will help you. Remember the question of Jesus, 'Do you want to get well?' See ya."

Clarke felt like Dustin Hoffman in the film *Papillon*, left on an island to roam free until he died, except in this case boredom would be the killer. He had read the book twice already; the three sections were entitled, "From Relevance to Prayer," "From Popularity to Ministry," and "From

Leading to Being Led." It didn't seem relevant to him. He didn't care whether he was relevant, popular, or leading; he just wanted a beer.

He did reach one milestone, after being there four hours. Nouwen's words weren't doing much for him, but he couldn't forget the sister's little joke, "We will teach you to live without it." That made a lot of sense. He wondered, *How does that work?* He focused on the first part of her sentence, "If there is anything you think you need." Clarke thought he needed sex, booze, and the game, risk, thrill, whatever would keep the adrenaline flowing freely through his veins. The negotiations had begun.

✳ ✳ ✳

Jen shuddered when she saw an envelope in the mail like the one that had arrived a few days earlier. She almost didn't open it for fear of losing control. When she slid the pictures out of the envelope, her shaking hands dropped them in horror. They were all of her, shopping, running, stretching, some including Janie.

Across one was written, "Nice ass, great tits, soon they will be mine." Another said, "You're mine, bitch." The one with her on her hands and knees stretching said, "Thanks for getting in the right position, I'll be right there."

One struck horror in Jen. It showed her and Janie walking hand in hand into the grocery store: "First you, bitch, then the baby bitch."

Just then Jen heard the sound of shattering glass from the family room. She ran toward the back of the house and found herself in Antonio's grip, his powerful arms locked around hers as he clamped a hand over her mouth. He lifted her off the ground and took her, kicking wildly, into the bedroom. Jesús was there to greet her with a gag, which he taped over her mouth. It took both men and all their strength to get her tied down to the bedposts. Jen had heard their names, she knew who they were, but she wasn't sure why they were there. Her eyes bulged with fear as she continued to strain and pull on the ropes.

"Hey, bitch, now we'll see how brave your super pastor husband is. I'm going to lick you clean." Jesús wanted more than his money; he wanted to strike at Hart's core, and that was between his bitch's legs. Jesús got on the bed and straddled Jen. She closed her eyes and turned her head; her muffled screams were desperate. He took out a knife, cut off her jeans, and ripped off her shirt. He pulled down his pants and began to rub himself against her, when he felt Antonio's grip on his shoulder,

"Get off, get off her now!" Antonio's great strength pulled him right off the bed. "You can't do this; she's a preacher's wife. Let's get out of here." Antonio had his back up.

Jesús took one look at his friend's face and knew he would not back down. Jesús pulled up his pants and said, "Listen, bitch, tell your husband we want our money, all the money. No more games, or we'll be back."

Suddenly they were gone. Jen could hear the back door slam and she lay alone in silence. It took her thirty minutes to work herself loose and get to her phone.

She called Michael in tears. He didn't answer his cell. She didn't leave a message but immediately called Millie, composing herself. "Where is Michael? He's not answering his cell."

Millie could sense some tension in Jen's voice. "Everything all right, honey?" The way she asked told Jen that she knew all was not well.

"I can't talk right now, Millie. I just need to speak with Michael."

✳ ✳ ✳

Millie pressed mute and went to the door to interrupt Michael's meeting with the executive director of the Central Indiana Pregnancy Center. "Michael, I'm very sorry, but your wife needs to speak with you."

"Okay, tell her I will call her back in a few." He turned back around.

Millie stepped closer. "Michael, you need to take this call now; it sounds urgent." Michael seemed a bit irritated, but life had taught him to trust her.

"Sorry," he apologized to his guest. "I'll take the call, and then you can step back in my office in a moment." On his way out, Michael shook hands with his guest and apologized, but he soon learned he needed to leave immediately to address a family issue.

All the way home, Michael's emotions were trying to find a foundation, wandering all over his mind and soul. Who would be handling this matter, Pastor Michael Hart or a skilled assassin whose reputation was as the most efficient killer in naval history, someone so effective that he still was known as someone the country might call upon again if he were needed? He was considered by the high command as a possible leader to take out Osama bin Laden. But when it came down to it, there were others who could do that job. If there were delicate missions where an international figure had to go, but there couldn't be any evidence, any trail, then Captain Hart could be called again. The general consensus was that he was a happy man, a pastor; leave him alone. Jesús and Antonio weren't smart enough to leave the Reverend Michael Hart alone, so now they were about to meet Captain Hart.

— 10 —

Michael never thought he would go back into the life. He had left that life when he left the military. His understanding of violence was shaped by the great Dietrich Bonhoeffer, a German pastor who wanted to live as a pacifist but was executed for his part in a plot to assassinate Adolf Hitler. Life is messy.

Bonhoeffer's dilemma led him to write about levels of morality, "It is better to do evil than to be evil." Speaking of defending the Jews, Bonhoeffer wrote, "Not to speak is to speak, not to act is to act." Michael was confused, but he thought that dealing with Jesús and Antonio—and anyone that led to—in order to save his family was a moral act.

He pulled into his driveway, the garage door went up, and ten seconds later he was holding Jen. She seemed inconsolable, and soon his shirt was soaked with her tears. Over the next few minutes she was able to describe what had happened. Again and again, Michael embraced her as she struggled to explain her ordeal. Jen was coming apart. Over her shoulder his eyes went cold.

"What are we going to do, Michael?" She floated her idea: "I think we should call the police. Ken Bohannon could help us." Jen was grasping for any hope at all.

Michael shook his head sadly. "I don't think he can. I don't trust him, but I do trust you, and I am going to tell you something. You won't like it."

Jen wiped her tears away and looked at him intently.

"These men…I know their names, I know where they live. I know that, because Ken Bohannon knows them. In fact, I suspect he protects them, and he is taking money from their organization."

Jenny's face contorted. She was not sure whether to be

more upset that Michael knew all this and still let Corey play with Jerry, or that he knew that Bohannon was dirty. She didn't know what was real.

She stood up, walked away, and then turned in a fury. "Dammit, Michael, what else haven't you told me? It's only the life of our kids. It's only the trust we have that I have never questioned until now." Out of steam, she sank to the floor with a whimper. "How could you?"

Michael knelt beside her. "Jen, I haven't lied to you, I've protected you." Michael put his arms around her. "I would never betray you."

He drew a big breath and glanced at his watch. It would be another hour before one of them would need to pick up the kids and get them safely home.

"Jen, sit up here. I've got to tell you a bit more. I have a plan." He was about to cross a line that would test Jen's trust and change their lives forever.

"I've thought about this moment for a while; I was hoping it would never come. I can't go to the police. They can't help us yet. Bohannon would have no reason to help. If he helps me, he will be killed by those who run the two thugs who kidnapped the boys. They pay him for protection, and they are ruthless. You've seen the way the Mexicans handle the drug wars on the news—how many people get killed, how many decapitations, and so on. They are inhumane."

Jen spoke up, "Aren't there some honest cops? Can't you go to the mayor, the FBI, the military? You used to be in the Navy." She was straining for something she knew.

"All they can do is warn these men. We can't prove they are the ones who took the pictures unless we let the authorities in on our illegal activities in getting the boys back. If we identify them as your attackers, they will get very expensive legal counsel. It will force us to tell the story in court and expose our kids to it all. That would be worth it if it worked, but it won't solve the problem. It doesn't eliminate their bosses from getting involved from New York. These guys play by a different set of rules. If we take them through the courts, they will lawyer up and still come after us as a matter of machismo."

He was doing his best to explain to Jen and justify to himself what he was seeing clearly. He wasn't sure how to pray about this; his normally quick habit to pray was somehow turned off. Captain Michael Hart's mind was locked down on the plan.

"I'm afraid, Jen. These men will kill you, Corey, Janie. They will spare no one. I don't mean these two lowlifes, but their people." Michael didn't know about Alonzo yet, but he had known many other Alonzos, and he knew what he was dealing with.

"I've got a plan. I am going to take a month's sabbatical, and we are all getting out of here. I'm going to tuck you and the kids away with a guy I know in New Mexico. His name is Jack Larsen. He has a wife and a ranch outside Santa Fe, and you will be safe there. He is one of my old buds from the Navy; I trust him completely. I'm going to deal with these men the way I learned in the Navy."

He paused and looked at Jen intently in the hope she wouldn't pull away. "I was in Special Forces, not the Navy SEALS, but in a different unit that specialized in eliminating key figures in the opposition. We had no name, and no one has ever found out about us. We were and are so secret that still no one talks about us because they don't know about us. I am breaking the law by even telling you that I was a member.

"There is only one thing these maniacs understand, that they need to be as afraid of us as people are of them. I have a few friends that I can call on. We are going to take care of this, and then I'll come and get you."

She just sat there, not saying a word, and then she burst out laughing. "Michael"—she took his face into her hands—"is this real, is that you in there? It sounds like you, it looks like you, but is it you?"

He smiled. "Yes, Jen, it's me, your radio pastor, your televangelist, and your trained assassin; depends on what you need."

"What do you mean, 'take care of it'? You don't have a license to kill, do you?"

Michael hesitated. "I'm not sure what we will need to do, but whatever it is, we plan to get away with it. I plan to return home with you and the kids and continue on at the church."

Jen gave him that look again. "Do you know how crazy that sounds?" Her voice dripped with sarcasm. "One day you're preaching about loving and serving others as disciples of Jesus, and the next you're executing bad guys like you are playing a video game. No one finds out, and it's back to happy land. What is going on inside of you? Isn't there anything else?" She sat back, exhausted.

Michael laid it out straight: "We could wait here in the house until they come and get us. We could offer no resistance, practice what some people call the Jesus way, no fight back, no defense, perfect peacekeepers. 'Blessed are the peacemakers, for they will be called the children of God.' There are people, Jen, who believe—even Bonhoeffer wanted to believe it—that for the Christian to live completely free, he must turn all things over to Christ, even self-defense. They believe that evil will not be added to evil if there is nothing resisting evil. Evil will become powerless when it finds no opposing object. Evil comes to an end when we permit it to pass over us without defense.

"But Bonhoeffer couldn't live that ideal; he personally concluded that it was better to do evil than to be evil. God Himself must destroy evil; Lucifer and his minions will not respond to God's love. These men, Jen, are evil. Kindness will not appease them any more than it would the devil incarnate."

He took her by the shoulders. "Babe, it's not them or me; it's them or us. It's them or Corey and Janie, your parents, and any other friends who get in the way. Listen, I want you to get the kids ready to be gone for a month. We'll leave first thing Monday morning. We will complete our weekend services, I'll make an announcement, and we'll be off to New Mexico."

Jen nodded. Then she grabbed him by the neck, placing her forehead on his. "I don't want to know what you do, but Michael, you do whatever it takes. You end this. You have my blessing."

Tears rolled down his cheeks. He now sensed he was on a mission blessed by Jen, blessed by God. He sensed he had been anointed.

✳   ✳   ✳

Michael's first phone call was to Ron Walker, informing him that he, Jen, and the kids were leaving in two days for a one-month sabbatical.

The ink was not yet dry on the sabbatical white paper circulating through the personnel committee. Now the head guy wanted to test it out sooner than expected. Ron was okay with the abruptness. He sensed some edge to Michael and thought it might prove salutary. Just as in the coffee shop, Ron knew Michael was withholding. He recommended it be approved immediately by the board. An e-mail vote was taken, and everyone agreed. The next steps were to inform the staff and congregation.

On Friday afternoon, Michael called a staff meeting of all senior leaders and announced his month-long sabbatical for prayer, contemplation, rest, and preparing for his future. He even quoted an old bromide, "Come apart, or you will come apart." He received a standing ovation.

The only unanswered question that was on everyone's mind was "Why now, with no warning? Aren't your kids still in school?" Michael anticipated the concern and told everyone that homeschooling would be undertaken for the month and that he was resting and repairing for the New Year. He would be back in time to run the world outreach conference. Everyone thought it a bit odd; something was not quite right about the way the Harts rolled it out, but their closest friends sensed a disquieting tone to it all. Ron Walker's gut was tight; Michael's eyes had lost their softness, and his stare was a bit more blank, a little less engaged, a bit too robotic.

Michael toughed it out through the four weekend services, preaching to ten thousand live, another four thousand on satellite feed to distant sites, and of course many more thousands on delayed television and podcast. He did a marvelous job describing Elijah's battle with Jezebel and the prophets of Baal and his subsequent flight to Beersheba, that the prophet needed rest, food, and more rest. The angel fed Elijah and gave him enough food for strength to travel forty days to Mount Sinai, where God spoke to him in a quiet voice.

By the time he was finished, his many followers were absolutely convinced that the sabbatical was of God. It was a walk-off performance for Michael, and the room was on its feet. They were standing on campus, they were standing on the south side in Greenwood, on the east side in Speedway, and the far north in Anderson. Michael was off to see the Lord, and the congregation knew it was right.

— 11 —

Corey and Janie were still confused, but there they were, crammed into the Honda Pilot with Dad and Mom at 5:30 AM. Michael had hot coffee in hand as he blew past the airport on their way out I-74 toward Terre Haute and points west.

It was too early for Jesús and Antonio to even notice. Their surveillance was to start today as they would tighten the noose around Michael Hart's family. First they would squeeze Hart—not for ransom this time, just information on where Clarke was. Scare them, don't kill them. It was Clarke they wanted to kill. But with Michael and family gone, and Clarke reading his daily Nouwen, they were going to be very frustrated.

It would be a twenty-four-hour drive to Taos, New Mexico. That was why just outside Plainfield, a little west of Indianapolis, Michael pulled off on a side road and found the municipal airport. On the runway sat a small jet aircraft with the engine running. Jack Larsen walked down the steps of the plane and welcomed Michael with open arms.

"How's my boy?" Larsen actually lifted Michael off the ground; he was still very strong, stronger than his fifty-five years suggested. He was no longer the Captain of Captains. His hair, shoulder length, was now mixed with white and blond, and he sported a nice pointed beard.

"Ready to go, kids?" Jack had kids of his own, and he loved them, "We're going to fly to my ranch. We've got horses, lakes, beautiful mountains…you will love your vacation with Uncle Jack."

Jen was putting on the best face, hugging Uncle Jack, a man she had never met until now, never known he existed until a few hours earlier. She glanced at Michael, who nodded and smiled. "You couldn't be safer than with this man. I trust him completely. And he is capable of protecting you. He trained me. He was the best before he made me the best."

Jen knew that for Michael, best was not a theological category, but in this realm there needed to be a best. It gave her a sense of comfort. She grabbed Michael by his coat. "You come back to me, hear? You come back in one piece with this all done. I want to go back to our lives."

Michael knew only one thing to do. "I promise, Jen, I promise." Five minutes later, the plane was in the air, and Michael turned the Honda Pilot back toward Indianapolis.

Instead of turning north on I-465, Michael turned south and two hours later knocked on Clarke's guesthouse door. Clarke opened the door, thinking maybe it was a lonely sister with a stimulated libido.

"You've got to be kidding me." Clarke was surprised but happy to see his Moses come to lead him out of his exile. "What are you doing here already? Don't get me wrong, I'm happy to see you."

Michael laughed. "Enjoying it that much?" He couldn't resist pressing on: "Got Henri Nouwen memorized yet? He waited for a typical Tommy Boy response.

"He's a bit too gay for me—you know, the priesthood, his love for art. Did you know he wrote a complete book on one painting? I think it was called *The Return of the Prodigal.* I think that must be why you gave me the book; I'm your prodigal."

Michael smiled. "Not exactly, but I've come for you, Tom. We have gone mission critical." He brought Clarke up to speed, and forty minutes later they had a midmorning breakfast at a Denny's just south of Bloomington.

Clarke was wobbly on killing Jesús and Antonio. "Why not just hurt them, scare them back to New York?"

"Because they won't quit. They have lost face, honor, and they can't go back without a pound of flesh." Michael was passionate. "Also because they can fill everyone in on us—who we are, where we live—and they will come after our families because we have ruined their business in central Indiana. They don't care because they won't get caught. They have too many law enforcement people on their payroll. Bohannon might be one of many, we just don't know. You've seen the pictures; what else can I do?"

He leaned across the table. "Look, Tom, you got us into this mess. Now, you've got to help me get us out, clean." Even Clarke was stunned at the look in Michael's eyes. He had seen it before; Michael would not be denied.

"Tommy," Michael was intense, feeling his own insides churning, "these guys are evil. It is better to do evil than to be evil. This is the way to stop it."

Clarke was trapped. "Okay, let's do it, let's plan it."

— 12 —

Clarke drove a nondescript Chevy Malibu. It was what he had left from his divorce settlement. It looked like one of those cars that people leave beside the road when they are finished with it. It used to be an off-red, but now its color was more of a rust. They decided that it would be a perfect surveillance car; neither Antonio nor Jesús would notice it.

Michael wanted to know if they had any patterns. When did they get up and leave the house? Where did they get their groceries? Did they bring them in the front door or the back door?

For three days, Clarke observed their patterns. He reported, "They stay up late. They usually hit a sports bar for dinner and then go off to a movie or club." Clarke seemed bored by it all. "Other than that, they stay close to home. They seem to be working in the living room; they treat it like an office."

Michael had taken his own turn observing. "They seem to be lying low since they attacked Jen. They know I'm coming." Michael had delight in his eyes. He loved the idea of being back.

He went on, "We know they have handguns. I am sure they have some rifles, semiautomatic, but they're loan sharks, not soldiers for the Mexican Mafia. They probably don't have a lot of training with any of it." Michael was seething when he thought of Jesús with his hands on Jen's body. "We can expect them to have set some traps for us. Their weapons will be near them at all times."

It had been a long three days for Michael. He didn't like hotels, and he particularly didn't like the downtime. He had too much time to think.

Jen's words kept running through his mind: "How can you preach about love and forgiveness and then ponder killing people? What kind of example is that?" Her emotional words told him she didn't grasp some of life's hardest choices. It did feel wrong, but his training and logic told him it was a means of justice. He could wait for Jesús and Antonio to receive God's justice one day, but he wouldn't wait to remove them from the face of this earth because they were an imminent threat to his family.

He would usually snap back to attention after a long spell of introspection in order to notice what his foes were doing or the equipment he would need to buy. They decided to use some of Bohannon's cash. It served him right for taking it from the crooks anyway.

Michael didn't keep weapons in his home; neither did he store them at another site. For a man so accomplished with a variety of lethal tools, he owned none; he kept no souvenirs. In fact, he was a gun control advocate. He couldn't understand why any normal citizen would need an automatic weapon or assault rifle. Clarke had sold or gambled away all his rifles and knifes except one. He even had gotten five hundred dollars for his special Kevlar protective gear.

They dared not go into this without some weapons, though Michael saw no need of guns to get the job done. Clarke felt differently. He knew where to get a couple of SOG SEAL knives cheap. He was able to connect with an old Navy buddy, Randall Egan, a collector who sold them for a hundred each. Clarke did still have his rifle that he'd trained on Jesús the night of the kidnapping; what they needed were a couple of handguns.

Michael came around to Clarke's point of view, but he couldn't buy guns without ID, and at this point he didn't want registered guns. They would need to find illegal, unlicensed weapons.

Clarke's buddy came through again with the name of a local dealer who would part with a gun for a grotesque amount of money. After only twenty-four hours of searching, Michael met the guy, who served as a middleman to sell two Glock 17 semiautomatic pistols for a thousand apiece. No registration, no license, no trace back to seller or buyer.

Michael swallowed hard at the price and took the guns. They had two knives, two pistols, walkie-talkies, and some knowledge, enough to get it done. The fourth night was the night.

It was crisp enough that you could see your breath and feel the crunch of grass under your feet. They had parked the stolen Porsche 911 a block away, on a street parallel to Kingsley Drive. Michael and Clarke made their way down the alley flanked by backyards, garages, and every kind of fencing, security lights flashing, garbage cans, and the piercing eyes of cats and the indiscriminate barking of dogs.

Both were dressed in black from head to toe, including their Nike sporting gloves with the fluorescent swoosh blacked out. Michael carried only the SEAL knife and had the Glock tucked in the back of his trousers. Clarke donned a backpack that included cleaning fluid, cotton swabs, a few medical tools in case bullets would need to be excised from bodies or walls, and a couple of microfiber towels for cleaning surfaces without water. No one seemed to notice their movement. Most were asleep and used to thinking every bark and catfight was just some animal protecting and posturing for the long night ahead.

Michael hopped the chain-link fence and moved swiftly up the backyard to a lighted window. He could see Jesús putting away groceries; very domestic. Clarke arrived right beside him. Intent on finding the whereabouts of Antonio, he continued across the back of the house peeking in windows.

They could be grateful that Antonio and Jesús didn't have any pets or watchdogs. It was quiet, except that the little dachshund next door continued to bark. A man stuck his head out of the back door and yelled, "Choppo, get in here." The dog retreated into the house under protest.

Clarke came on the radio. "I've got him—front room, on the computer."

"Okay," Michael said, "plan 1. Go." With that, he went to a darkened window, one he had unlocked and lubricated earlier in the day when Antonio and Jesús were out. He lifted the window and slipped into the unused back room. The beauty of it was that the Mexican boys loved their music very loud. With their favorite mix playing, Michael could have fallen through the window, and no one would have heard him.

Just then, there was a pounding on the front door. It was an irate neighbor there to complain about the loud music being played at 2:15 AM. Jesús and Antonio were night owls; that was when they were at their creepy best.

Antonio peeked out and saw the angry look on the dachshund owner's face. Now that his dog had gotten him up, he was going to give Cheech and Chong a piece of his mind.

Antonio opened the door. "Do you know what time it is, son?" The look on his neighbor's face almost made Antonio burst out laughing. "Turn that damn music down, or I'm calling the cops."

Antonio apologized, "Sir, I'm sorry. We will turn it down. Now get the hell out of here."

With that, the neighbor left, grumbling, and shuffled back into his house. Clarke decided to call an audible; sometimes fate just smiles on you. He made his way to the porch and pounded on the front door. Antonio yelled, "What?" ran to the door, and yanked it open. His brain didn't have time to register danger before the butt of

Clarke's gun knocked him out. Clarke was in.

Michael heard it and moved into the hallway. Jesús heard some noise and entered the hallway from the kitchen. He saw Michael and ran away toward the back door. He had barely opened the door when Michael caught him and plunged the knife into his throat. Jesús didn't make a sound; Captain Hart was his old efficient self.

Antonio was waking up, still a bit fuzzy, but he scrambled to his feet. Clarke grabbed him, but Antonio's strength was enough to slam him to the floor. Antonio stepped into the hallway, looking for Jesús, so Michael came through the kitchen and stepped in behind Antonio. It was over in an instant, with no sound but the plunge of the knife into the jugular with a hand over the mouth. He slowly laid Antonio down on the hallway floor.

The deed was done. Michael checked the scene for any interesting papers, taking the computers, cell phones, and one iPad, after checking the printer. Clarke started his cleaning. He turned off the music and intentionally left wallets on their victims so the police would be able to trace them to New York City and Alonzo. He wiped the surfaces clean of any fibers or evidence that could be traced to them.

Michael turned off the kitchen light and exited the house; he would go back to the car first. Soon Clarke finished his work, turned off all the lights, and followed. They sped out of the sleeping neighborhood. The dachshund's owner rolled over in bed with a smile on his face. The music had stopped, and Cheech and Chong's lights were off. "Now maybe I can get some sleep."

— 13 —

Jerry Revis wasn't feeling so good with last night's dinner at the in-laws' still crawling around his insides. His wife, Mary, always insisted they eat at her mother's house on her birthday. It was that damn taco casserole from hell that always multiplied in weight overnight in the gut that forced Jerry to skip his morning bear claw and order an extra large black coffee at Dunkin' Donuts.

Jerry's partner, Johnny "Puke" Johnson, was scarfing down two plain cake donuts, advertised as gluten-free; he was on a diet. Puke got the name for losing his lunch at his own wedding just as he and his bride were pronounced husband and wife. It was funny how some things stuck with you when other things didn't.

Jerry and Puke were not Robocops; they couldn't sprint one block given their breakfast routine, pot bellies, and the cigarettes falling out of their pockets. Both their wives sent lunch with them, but most days they threw it in the trash and had a burger. Fourteen and ten years, respectively, as Marion County sheriffs had made them suspicious, cynical, and smart in the ways of the world.

"Can't believe how good this rookie quarterback is doing." Puke was a rabid Colts fan.

"Yeah, but he's got a lot to learn." Jerry fought back the acid reflux. Just then, he felt something and realized it was his phone, not his stomach.

"This is Revis." Puke looked up from the paper. "Okay, we got it."

"What is it?" Puke folded the paper and stood to leave.

Revis sighed. "Got two dead bodies. A gardener found them. Kingsley Drive, 4929."

"I know that neighborhood. My nephew went to Public School 91 near there." Puke turned the car south down Meridian toward 49th Street.

It was an old neighborhood, typical white middle class in the 1950s, but now a mix of working-class whites, on-the-move Asians, blacks, and Hispanics. Revis and Puke made their way past the uniformed officers and walked in the front room of the two-storied Craftsman home.

The first victim was identified as Antonio Sanchez, forty, of New York City. He had no cuts or abrasions except for the well-placed slash across his neck and a small contusion on his forehead. There were no signs of a struggle. It was as though someone had come up from behind and ended it quickly.

"Let's see the other one," Revis said as he turned to walk away. The second victim was Jesús Alvarez, thirty-one, also of New York City. He was lying on the back steps, his body holding open the screen door. Again, there were no signs of struggle; it was as if whoever did this had done it quickly, quietly, and laid down his prey gently on his back. Revis wondered if he was opening the door or running out the door. Both men were Hispanic, in good shape, and in their underwear.

Puke laid out his homespun analysis. "Looks like the boys heard some noise, and then the angel of death did his thing."

Jerry Revis had seen crime scenes before. Rarely had he seen one with two murder victims with so little evidence: no prints, no signs of break-in. The killer or killers had taken the victims' cell phones and computers but left a small arsenal of handguns and their wallets with driver's licenses; hence the easy identification. "Looks like they wanted us to know they were dangerous guys up to no good." Puke had the gift for the obvious, an important skill in an investigator.

It was easy for people to think police work was like the

CSI TV series, that experts and a crime lab were always available to make it all work. But Revis knew that kind of budget and personnel were not easy to come by. About thirty police officers were crawling all over the house and yard, and the uniforms were going door to door.

Revis cleared his throat. "I would say these two guys from New York were dirty. They had very little furniture, and what was there was rented. They hadn't been here long enough to remove the plastic wrap, but they were planning on being here a while." He stopped talking and sighed.

"The crime lab boys and girls have found some stuff for us to look at." Puke waved Jerry over to a table filled with collected papers, food wrappers, utility bills, jewelry, and other items.

"We will find out later, but it looks like their last meal was Chipotle." Puke ran his latex glove across the wrapper and captured a dab of the bean burrito.

"Yeah," said Revis, "guess this is the new generation Latino, gourmet Mexican food rather than traditional. That's one of the stops we'll need to make."

Mary Eagan from the coroner's office came over and said, "They've been dead since about two this morning, give or take an hour. Death was instantaneous, and it was done with a serrated blade. Whoever did this knew how to be lethal in a very small space. It wasn't messy, and it was quick."

Revis looked at Puke. "So we have two thugs on assignment from New York who are setting up housekeeping in Indy, and they end up dead, killed by a professional. Why?"

Puke laughed. "I wonder if it's about drugs or money?"

"All right." Jerry was starting to feel better now. "We have a lot of work to do. They took the cell phones because Frick and Frack here must have talked about them with someone. They may have mentioned the killer's name or someone who sent the killer. They don't want it traced back. We need to find out who these guys worked for, and then we might be able to figure this out."

It was late afternoon by the time Revis and Puke got back to their station at 92nd and Meridian. Revis's lunch, compliments of his wife, was already doing its work. He was headed for the men's room. Puke, who knew better than to even look in his lunch sack, lobbed it into the trash and was slurping on the last of his Peanut Butter Moo'd energy drink.

"Hey, Puke, still on that diet?" laughed Lieutenant Kenny Bohannon.

"Very funny," Puke said, not even looking at him.

"Where you been all day? Did you and Revis take in a good movie, a long lunch, and a stroll through the mall hand in hand?"

Bohannon waited for an answer. Puke looked up and turned toward Bohannon. "If you must know, Kenny Boy, we caught a couple of dead Mexicans from NYC that were executed in the night over on Kingsley Drive."

A chill went down Bohannon's spine. He laughed, but with that look that one gets when they think their fart was too real. "Got to have a smoke," he said and left the building.

Outside, Bohannon leaned against the brick wall and exhaled. He hadn't counted on this.

He first met Alonzo Alvarez when he was seventeen, a high school dropout with a small tattoo on his right deltoid and Lucky Strikes rolled up in his shirtsleeve. If someone ever rolled off the screen on a motorcycle from the movie *Grease*, it was Kenny Bohannon.

He had yellow curly hair, his scrawny body draped in black leather jeans. His boots and jacket were tight and alternative; the other main thing he owned was a bad attitude. He was headed nowhere on that Harley except possibly jail. That was where Kenny's daddy already was; he might as well join him there.

Robert Bohannon, or "Daddy," had headed up Alonzo Alvarez's Indiana satellite drug operation and had become a trusted friend of Alvarez. "Daddy" Bohannon was the only white "made man" in the Mexican Mafia, a brother in arms. When the Indiana operation was exposed, Bohannon kept the code of silence and started doing hard time in Michigan City. For that AA was grateful, and for that reason he promised to take care of Kenny.

He got Kenny a high school diploma, got him into Ball State, and later got him an appointment to the Marion County Sheriff's Department. And for that Kenny was grateful because not only did it give him a career, but AA took care of his mother and saw to it that his two brothers and sister, who were better students, got into Indiana University in Bloomington.

Kenny had promised AA that he would take care of Jesús and Antonio, keep the cops away, and make sure AA's wayward baby brother would stay out of trouble. Kenny had even told Jesús about a good place to rent furniture and how to move into a nondescript neighborhood where no one would notice them. He even sent his own gardener to keep up the place.

And now he was dead. *Oh shit*, Bohannon thought; there would be hell to pay. He would need to stay close to Revis and Puke to find out what they knew. He knew he would be responsible for learning who killed Jesús and telling Alonzo. This was the kind of thing Alonzo liked to take care of himself.

*　＊　＊　＊*

Michael left the cleanly scrubbed Porsche 911 alongside the northbound lanes of Interstate 69 toward Fort Wayne.

After some fitful sleep and breakfast, he and Clarke raced south in Jen's Honda Pilot to return Clarke to his spiritual retreat with the sisters and more Henri Nouwen readings about peace and love. Michael thought this would be the best place to deposit his unpredictable friend.

Clarke put things in focus. "I can't believe this just happened, Michael. We were two college guys doing Bible study and chemistry, and now we are in deep shit."

Michael wasn't ready to laugh. "You just stay here. Don't make calls; don't expect to hear from me for up to a month. Do you hear me, man?" He was committed to getting away with this; it was vital to his plan.

Just then, Michael's phone rang through the synced Bluetooth in his car's system. The screen readout said Ken Bohannon. Michael put his finger to his mouth to tell Clarke to be quiet, hit the answer button on the steering wheel, and did his best to sound upbeat.

"Hey, Lieutenant, what's up?" At once he went on, "I'm not sure you know, Ken, that I am on a sabbatical and not in town. What can I do for you?"

Bohannon spit it out: "Michael, we found two dead men in a house on Kingsley Drive earlier today. You have met these two men, Jesús Alvarez, thirty-one, and Antonio Sanchez, forty. Their throats were cut, and there is very little evidence. You wouldn't know anything about the death of these guys, would you?"

Michael waited a beat. "Like I said, Ken, I'm not in Indianapolis. I am away in an undisclosed location. How could I know about it?"

Bohannon was unsatisfied; he needed to question Michael more without revealing their mutual knowledge of the victims. Since all phone calls were recorded, it must be proper.

"Michael, you had a motive, and certainly your friend Tom Clarke has an even better reason to want these guys dead. Do you happen to know what's happened to Clarke? We would like to question him, at least the guys who are conducting the investigation."

"Wait a minute, Ken." Bohannon sensed Michael was about to say something he didn't want recorded, so he turned off the record button.

He was right. Michael did get real: "You have a motive as well. In fact it would be interesting for your bosses to know your connection to these two men. The only reason you had all that cash when they took the boys was because you are dirty, because you took money to protect the kingpin's baby brother. You might remember we talked about that the first time we met and you sent me their names and address."

Michael went on, "I would now expect you to call your real boss in New York, and you will deflect blame and give him my name and Clarke's name and probably tell them where we live. Then he will send his people to kill all of us—you, me, our families, Clarke. They don't leave witnesses or loose ends."

Bohannon was cornered. He cleared his throat. "What would be your recommendation? If I protect you, I'm dead; if I expose you, I'm what?"

Bohannon wasn't the sharpest knife in the drawer. "Either way you're probably dead or in jail, Kenny." Michael paused. "I do have one recommendation. Tell Alonzo Alvarez his brother is dead and that you don't know who did it. If he thinks it was us, which I'm sure he will, he'll send someone to look for us. At present they won't find me because I'm gone. They will look for Clarke. When they don't find Clarke, that's when I am worried for you.

"Make the investigators work at it. All I want from you is the whereabouts of Alvarez. It is easier to defend yourself if you know what direction your enemy is coming from. It will take your investigators a bit of time to contact me for questioning, so if you keep your mouth shut, we might be able to find a way to bring this to a good end."

Bohannon was silent, his mind churning as fast as a challenged brain could work. He finally spoke. "Okay, I'll try that, but if he blames me, I'll need to run for cover, and that includes my ex and the boys."

Michael's mind was geared up to give advice. "Kenny, if you have ever prayed, now is the time." He pushed end call. He wondered what God must be thinking. *I'm praying, and I just killed two men. A dirty cop is praying that his lie will be believed by a very religious kingpin who crosses himself before he kills. Just another day for God, not that God lives in days.* As Augustine demonstrated in his *Confessions*, the inventor of time is not a captive of time.

— 14 —

Alonzo Alvarez rolled over in bed only to find another naked woman. His head was a bit fuzzy; the many nights and the women, drugs, and alcohol that filled them all ran together. They never looked as young or flawless in bright morning sun as the night before. He would roll out of bed and shower, and by the time he finished breakfast, José, his valet, would have ushered her out of the penthouse. Alonzo never liked to talk to them sober. He seemed to be better with women when his judgment was impaired.

It had been a week since he had heard from Jesús. He felt calm as he read the *International Herald Tribune*. He fiddled with his poached eggs on a dry piece of toast. *How is this food?* He just couldn't get used to the nutritional life, but the doctors had ordered him to change his diet. He was over fifty and worth eleven billion dollars, and life was stressful, especially for those who worked for him—and deadly for those who opposed him.

He didn't read much, but he loved to study powerful men, especially unconventional ones like Stalin, Mao, and Castro. Keeping up with Alvarez was like keeping up with Stalin. Stalin was infamous for all-night drinking binges and getting rid of anyone who couldn't keep up. Stalin would go to bed in a different room every night and sleep until noon. His minions would stay up into the wee hours drinking, but instead of sleeping, they would need to rise early because Stalin would require reports of their work when he arose from his drunken stupor.

This was the curse on Alvarez's entourage. Poached eggs at 12:30 PM were followed immediately by a complete briefing on all his interests around the world. He wanted to know about the casinos in Monte Carlo, Kiev, Moscow,

Istanbul, and London, and even the ones in Oklahoma and Illinois that he owned under an alias. Next came the fashion houses in Paris, Milan, and Singapore. It took two hours to brief him and answer his questions.

Any reports on his covert work were handled through his New York office, which existed in the minds of his middle brothers Franco and Carlos. They worked wherever they were with laptops and cell phones, whether in their SUVs or a few bars and restaurants the family owned. He didn't like to be interrupted but had left an order with his assistant to take any call about Jesús.

The good lieutenant's hand shook a bit as he dialed Alonzo's number. What would he do? Kenny knew that Alonzo could be unpredictable; that was when he was the most dangerous.

Alonzo's assistant brought the mobile phone to him and whispered that it was about Jesús. Alonzo excused himself to the balcony overlooking Istanbul's Hippodrome with the Hagia Sophia at one end and the Blue Mosque at the other. He always found scenic balconies safe places for private conversation. "Well, Kenny, has my wayward brother found his way home to New York yet?" He felt upbeat and wasn't prepared for Kenny's tone.

"Alonzo"—Kenny's somber voice wiped the smile from Alonzo's face—"I have some bad news. Jesús is dead; so is Antonio. Someone broke into their house and killed them."

Alonzo's mind went numb. He heard buzzing in his head and fell into the chaise lounge, almost passing out. He collected himself to say, "Who did it? How did this happen?"

This was Bohannon's first test. He was pretty sure Michael had done it, but had no proof and certainly no confession. "I am not sure; it could've been a rival outfit or some local wise guys who didn't like them setting up business here." Bohannon held his breath.

Alonzo felt anger, but experience helped him focus. "No one would dare hurt my brother. Every crook in that hick town knows me and knows that I could and would wipe out their families."

Bohannon gave an "uh huh."

Alonzo was homing in. "It had to be those two guys. The ones they had the conflict with, Hart and Clarke, the names you gave me before."

Bohannon tried something else: "One is a preacher—highly unlikely, Alonzo."

Alonzo wasn't convinced. "Listen, the preacher was able to hurt them. He was crafty enough to get his son back. This is no normal preacher. I want his address, and run a background check; you owe me at least that, Kenny."

Alonzo drew a breath and his voice changed. It might have been echoing from an open grave. "You failed me. You were supposed to protect them. I'm angry with you. I hope I don't learn anything about you having a part in this or protecting these men."

Bohannon knew the clock was ticking. It would only take a day or two for Alonzo's men to arrive in Indianapolis. They would be looking for Hart and Clarke, and of course they would be visiting him. It was time to run or at least to consider how to survive.

*　*　*

Michael Hart knew how to be anonymous. First, stay out of your home area, which meant not to return home or be seen in Indiana. Since Bohannon would not have told his investigators about the kidnapping or his own contact with the dead men, they were not looking for him. He needed to lay low, so he drove to Louisville and stayed at a nondescript Hampton Inn just off Interstate 65. He knew it was only a matter of time before Alonzo's men put the pressure on Bohannon and he gave them up.

Michael needed to locate Alonzo Alvarez. He knew his only hope for freedom was to cut the beast off at the head. New York was the man's home, so he called Joey Ludwig for help. Between Joey and Jack Larsen and even Tom Clarke calling in a few markers, they could find anyone anywhere. Whenever he could find Alonzo Alvarez, he would end it all.

— 15 —

It was unusual for Franco and Carlos to go on such an assignment. They were wiser and smarter than Jesús, but they had sent many a person into the next life, so Alonzo wanted them to handle it. This was personal; this was family.

They arrived at Indianapolis International Airport. Franco was amused by the *International* tag. "What's that about? It must be because they have a flight to Fort Wayne."

Carlos was used to his brother's bad jokes. "Yeah, let's take care of business and get out of Cornpone, USA." Their Hertz Gold Club reservation SUV was ready under the name of Jimenez. They remembered their friends telling them about the funny comedian Bill Dana's Man on the Street character, José Jimenez, on the *Steve Allen Show*.

They had three names: Ken Bohannon, Michael Hart, and Tom Clarke. Within two hours, they knew that Michael Hart was away on a sabbatical. They learned that when they called the church and asked to speak with him. After they found no one home at Tom Clarke's house, and neighbors told them he hadn't been around in a while, they decided to visit the good Lieutenant Bohannon.

He lived in a duplex just off Road 100 or 86th Street, close to old 421. It was a vintage 1970s one bedroom, one bath, one kitchen, one living room, all set off a long hallway. The outside was white wood lap sided and adorned with brick halfway up. It was the kind of place you lived in on your way up or your way down.

When Bohannon peeked out the door, he recognized Carlos and Franco, from their days together as boys when Kenny's father worked for Alonzo. He also knew they'd grown up to be very bad men when they had to be.

He opened the door. "Hey, boys, been a while. Come on in." Bohannon gave the appearance of a confident officer, but he was churning inside.

"Kenny, what happened to you?" Carlos laughed. "Christ, what a dump."

"Divorce, boys, divorce," Kenny chuckled. "She got the house, the kids, and the money." Franco and Carlos sat down and continued to look around in awe of how a police lieutenant lived.

Franco got to the point. "Kenny, where are the men who killed our brother?"

Kenny gave his standard answer. "I'm not sure who did it, but we have two detectives leading the investigation."

Franco laughed and shook his head. "Okay, Kenny, you know more. We heard about the kidnapping, how Jesús screwed that up, and how they beat the crap out of Antonio and Jesús. Anyone who knows Antonio knows he was one tough dude. I've never known anyone to get the best of him. Yet this preacher rung him up like he was a helpless kid."

Carlos's anger was building. "Listen, asshole, tell us where these two guys are, the preacher and the one who owes us money."

Bohannon shrugged. "I don't know, no clue."

Carlos stood and walked over to him. Bohannon sat calmly on the couch, comforted by the feel of his service revolver tucked between his shirt and sweater. "What do we need to do, Kenny, before you tell us the truth?" He was now leaning over Bohannon. Kenny tried to stand, but Carlos pushed him back onto the couch and pulled an ultralight .38 revolver out of his jacket before Bohannon could react. In an instant, Franco was helping Carlos keep Bohannon down.

The lieutenant reached for his own gun, but Carlos rammed the gun into Bohannon's temple. "Tell us what we want to know, Kenny, right now."

Bohannon began to sweat, barely keeping his composure. "I don't know where they are, I really don't. You have to believe me."

Carlos was at the end of his rope. He picked up Bohannon off the couch and pushed him down the narrow hallway into the bathroom. It was then that Bohannon reached for his gun, but it was too late. Franco saw it and swatted it away as they together threw the lieutenant into the bathtub. Carlos began to slam Bohannon's head against the tub. Franco was kicking and hitting him with his gun, while Bohannon kept yelling, "I don't know where they are!"

Franco stood up. "I don't think he knows." He pulled the trigger twice, and Lieutenant Kenneth Bohannon was dead.

Both Carlos and Franco knew they had overreached; it wouldn't be the first or the last time. But this was about family. Bohannon hadn't protected their brother; he deserved it.

They left the duplex without fanfare and returned to their room at the Keystone Crossing Raddison, having just killed their best source. But a source is not a source if he isn't talking or doesn't know. Yes, Bohannon was a longtime acquaintance, but he wasn't blood, he wasn't family. When a source is not a source, he can only be a witness. They needed a live source or a dead witness; the dead witness was the only kind the Alvarez family liked.

They decided to claim Jesús' body to send back to New York. Carlos and Franco drove to the city morgue to identify the body for transport. The coroner had strict orders not to release the body until the investigative officers could question whoever claimed it. When the Alvarez brothers showed their New York driver's licenses to the receptionist, he buzzed the assistant coroner on duty. He immediately called the police from his office; Revis and Puke were out the door and on their way.

James Burns had been assistant coroner for Marion County for twenty years, the kind of classic number-two man that makes organizations work well or sink into ineptitude. Now in his late fifties, he looked very important in his white medical coat, reading glasses parked on the end of his nose.

He entered the reception area and introduced himself to Franco and Carlos. "Good morning, gentlemen. I am Dr. James Burns. I'm glad you have come. We know this can be a very difficult thing for a family to do. For that reason we have a viewing room from which you can see the body, or if you like, we can go straight into the morgue and see the body live."

Franco was sure. "We want to see his body live."

Carlos agreed: "Yeah, live, up close."

Burns pointed toward the double steel doors. "Very well, gentlemen, follow me." He led Jesús Mario Alvarez's older brothers down a long hallway into a spacious refrigerated room, both walls lined with large drawers, each with a number. The doctor pulled out drawer 159, and there was Jesús. There was barely a mark on his body except the gash across his neck that had killed him.

Carlos was the first to break down. He and Franco touched their brother's remains, tears flowing. They both crossed themselves and then stepped back.

Dr. Burns spoke carefully: "We would like you to identify the body as that of Jesús Mario Alvarez, thirty-one, of New York City."

Both brothers nodded. Franco said, "That's him."

Carlos asked, "When will he be ready for transport?"

Burns had a great deal of experience. "Gentlemen, normally the remains are transported to a mortuary for preparation. A coffin is generally the best mode of transportation."

"How long with that take?" Carlos seemed anxious.

Burns stuck to business: "There are some administrative details, signing of documents, and of course we must complete the police report. You men will be able to see that report as soon as they close the investigation. Detectives Revis and Johnson will be here momentarily, and then we can release the body." The brothers looked at each other. "It's just routine in murder cases; it won't take long." He patted Carlos on the back and started to walk away, saying, "You can just wait here."

And with that, Carlos and Franco sat down, and Dr. Burns was gone. Carlos whispered to Franco, "They don't know anything about Bohannon. They only want to talk about Jesús and Antonio. Just stay calm."

A few minutes later, Revis and Puke walked in. They came over to the brothers, and Revis stuck out his hand. "Hello, gentlemen. We are sorry for your loss. I am Detective Jerry Revis of the Marion County Sheriff's Department, and this is my partner, John Johnson."

Franco and Carlos stood, shook hands, and seemed relaxed to Revis. The first thing Puke noticed were the expensive clothes the brothers wore: Prada shoes, Façonnable sweaters, and Ralph Lauren jeans. Not that Puke had ever shopped anywhere but Sears and Penney's, but he was paid to notice such things. Puke liked to get his shoes at the same store where he got his tires.

Revis started with the easy questions. "Your names are Franco and Carlos, and the deceased was your brother Jesús, is that right?"

After they nodded, he went on, "Do you know why anyone would want to kill your brother? Did he have enemies?" Puke almost snickered when Revis asked the question.

"We live in New York. We don't really know—we don't know anyone here; we have no idea." Carlos was first hesitant and then emphatic.

Puke chimed in, "Someone slipped into their house after 2:00 AM and slit their throats. Doesn't that sound planned or with malice?"

"My brother said we don't know!" Franco seemed a bit red in the face.

"What was your brother's business? Doesn't he work for your family?" Revis tightened the noose. "According to our inquiries, the Alvarez family has businesses around the world. Your older brother, Alonzo, is CEO. Wasn't your younger brother sent out here to open up an unconventional bank? Special customers with special rates?"

Franco's face expressed the rise in his temperature until Carlos put a hand on his knee. "Like we said, if he was sent out by our brother to do work, they didn't tell us about it. We are as much in the dark as you. Jesús was young and naïve. Antonio was a close friend. We have lost a lot, and we just want to go home."

Revis and Puke knew they were dirty; their brother had screwed up somehow and was killed for it. But there was no evidence. Revis wasn't finished, however: "Our records show that you both have been arrested several times for everything from DUI to assault and battery—with no convictions, just a few fines. The kinds of crime associated with loan sharking. It seems like your family has gone largely legit, but you still can't kick the habit. You still have a little crime syndicate left in your blood.

"People get killed in your line of work. Your brother Jesús, however, seemed to be the problem child. At least he got into more trouble: alleged rapes, destruction of property, income tax evasion, and then the everyday petty crime associated with your family." Revis waited for the brothers to react.

Carlos smiled. "Detective, do you have any reason to keep us here or ask more questions? We are anxious to get our brother back to New York."

Puke, not known for his genteel manner, said, "You guys know that we know something is dirty here. We have your information, so I suppose we'll sign the papers, and you can take Jesús home." Detective John Johnson turned and stepped out of the room before he said more.

Revis signed the release form. Then he turned to leave but had one last question. "You guys wouldn't be in town for another reason, would you?—like revenge or settling the score?"

Carlos realized that it was time to leave. "No comment, Detective." Carlos turned toward the desk to check how long before they could get the body.

As Revis and Puke walked to their car, Revis's phone vibrated, "Yeah, who is it?"

"Don't bite my head off. This is Jenna back at the station. No one has seen Ken Bohannon for two days. When he didn't report in this morning, we sent over a car. He was found dead in his bathtub; you need to get over there." Revis said nothing, ending the call.

"What was that? You look like you've seen a ghost."

Revis looked at Puke. "Ken Bohannon was just found dead in his bathtub. We've got to get over there."

"Holy shit, what is going on here?" Puke turned on the siren and floored it.

Bohannon's face was covered with blood, his scrawny body twisted into a lump like he was meant to sleep in the tub. The cocky young investigator from the coroner's office said death came around 10:00 that morning. Cause of death was two gunshots from a .38 caliber revolver, but it looked like that was preceded by blunt trauma to the head. Bohannon's service revolver was found in the hallway and had not been fired. They would check for prints, and the forensic team was combing the duplex.

"Who would need to kill Kenny?" Puke wondered out

loud to Revis. "His ex-wife didn't much care for him, but she's a churchgoing woman, and he paid child support for the two kids. That doesn't make sense."

Just then, an officer handed Revis a package. "What's this?" He opened the package and saw a lot of money. After thumbing through it, he estimated over fifty thousand dollars in twenties and hundreds.

"Kenny often spoke about being behind in alimony and child support and not having enough money. Obviously he was lying." Revis looked at Puke and sighed. "This isn't going to be pretty. Let these people finish their work. We'll get some reports. We need to go tell Sally what happened here."

※　※　※

Sally Bohannon had seen it on TV, two police officers walking somberly up to a slain officer's home.

Revis spoke first: "Sally, I don't know if you remember me. I'm Jerry Revis. We've met a few functions. Can Detective Johnson and I come in?"

Sally knew something was wrong. She opened the door and led them into her little-used sitting room. She couldn't hold it in. "What's wrong? Something has happened to Kenny, hasn't it?"

The next few minutes were torturous. Sally sobbed, she laughed; her mind flashed back to young Kenny's smiling face, their wedding, their children, the other women, a historic panorama speeding through her brain. She didn't feel divorced at the moment; it felt like her husband had died. Once she was able to catch herself, realizing she wasn't actually married and why she was no longer married to Kenny, a calm began to settle into her spirit.

"He was murdered? Was he on duty? What happened?"

Revis was brief. "We don't know who did it, but he was shot in his home. We are investigating." He took a deep breath. "Do you know any reason why someone would want to kill Kenny?"

Sally looked at Revis with a smirk. "I've wanted to kill him many times."

"Haven't we all?" Puke's awkwardness seemed to meet the need of the moment.

Sally interrupted, "I don't think it would hurt anything to tell you now about the kidnapping."

"What kidnapping?" Revis was surprised.

"You know those two Mexican Mafia types from New York City who were killed recently? They kidnapped my Jerry and Reverend Michael Hart's boy, Corey. Took them right off the school bus and asked for a ransom. It only lasted seven hours until Pastor Michael, Ken, and Pastor Michael's friend, Tom Clarke, gave them the money and they let the boys go."

Revis was trying not to show his shock. Puke looked at him and took a turn: "Why didn't they call the police?"

"Ken, Michael, and Tom decided to handle it themselves, didn't want any headlines; that would not be good for any of them. It turned out that Kenny knew Jesús and his family. Ken's father worked for that family many years ago. When Kenny's father died, Alonzo agreed to take care of Kenny until he was an adult.

"So Kenny helped Jesús and his friend find a place to live and get set up here in town. He didn't want you or anyone to know about that friendship. I didn't know any of this until the kidnapping. That's when Kenny explained it to me."

Revis and Puke just looked at each other. Revis was feeling confused. He asked, "If they got their money, why didn't they just go away, end of story?"

"I don't know. I do know that it all started with them

loaning money to Tom Clarke and his not being able to pay the money back. Pastor Michael was only involved because he and Tom are old friends, and Tom goes to the church. And then, of course, because they took Corey."

Revis was writing fast. "Why would they take Corey?"

"Because one night Jesús and his friend jumped Michael and Tom in a parking lot, and Michael beat up Jesús and the other guy pretty bad. They couldn't find Tom; he was hiding. Michael was the only one they could find, so they wanted to scare Michael. In the end, I think Michael scammed them, and they were very unhappy. That must have been when they attacked Jen, Michael's wife, in her own home. It was so traumatic that the whole family left a few days ago on a well-deserved sabbatical."

"Do you know where they went?" Revis had his pencil ready.

"No, I don't. Someone at the church may know, but I don't."

Revis stood and gave her a hug. "We are so sorry. I might need to talk with you again, but that's it for now. I know you will need to tell the kids. The department has all kinds of resources, and we want to provide any of them you might need." With that, Revis and Puke went to their car.

"Christ on a crutch, are you believing this?" Puke slapped his forehead in wonder. "Kenny was helping the mob, he doesn't tell us about the kidnapping, and the most Reverend Michael Hart is some kind of street fighter. I need a drink."

"At least we have a suspect for who killed Jesús and Antonio." Revis was still trying to grasp it. "He and this guy Clarke had a motive. Having your wife attacked in your own home is a good reason to want to kill someone, but to get from thinking about it to execution and the guts to do it—it's a stretch to believe Hart did it."

Since they were on duty, unlike *Masterpiece Theater's*

Inspector Morse and his assistant, Lewis, who would down a pint in an Oxford pub, Revis and Puke had to settle for an Americano at Starbucks. Puke was a funny guy; it would hurt his persona for people to think he was thoughtful. But truth be known, often it was he, Johnny Johnson, who would come up with the insight to solve a case.

"Let's say that Hart and Clarke did kill them. Then the head of the organization in New York City sends some thugs out to deal with the problem, to do 'research.' And those two guys can't find Hart or Clarke, so they go and visit Kenny, since they know him. They end up killing him and go to the morgue to claim the body of their brother, and we just happen to meet them. Hart and Clarke killed Jesús and Antonio, so Carlos and Franco kill Kenny."

Revis shrugged. "Nice, Puke. Too bad we can't prove it. But I'd sure like to talk to Michael Hart and this Clarke character—and Jennifer Hart, if we can find out where they are."

— 16 —

Michael was finding it hard to pray. He had always preached the value of silence and solitude, but lying low was proving to be too much of both. Jesus was led by the Spirit into the wilderness in order to be tempted by the devil; there he fasted forty days. Michael was only on his fifth day, and the heavens seemed shut.

He wondered how to pray about his intention to work his way up the Alvarez family tree until he cut off the head. How did the great warriors like David reconcile loving others and the necessities of war? Everybody gets David killing Goliath; he was mean and ugly and taunted God. But one wonders about him having Uriah killed to cover up his affair with Bathsheba. Yet he was known as a man after God's own heart. For that matter, how did God reconcile his care of people, yet gave his order to slay every living creature in cities like Jericho?

Michael was looking for his place in all this. His conscience wasn't clear, but his mind was made up. He asked himself over and over, *To what kind of God or to whom am I praying? I am praying to a God who has ordered mass killings. In today's world, He would be put on trial at The Hague for war crimes. If my God can be a warrior in certain contexts, then why can't I be a warrior in mine?*

After years of calling on God to heal the sick, to help the weak, to save souls, what did a prayer sound like that asked for special favor in killing a family? Praying, "Lord, give me intelligence, give me quickness of hand and mind in order to eliminate this evil." He kept going back to Bonhoeffer's struggle with his pacifist leanings and the necessity of killing Hitler: "It is better to do evil than to be evil." Yet Michael didn't think it was doing evil to eliminate a source of evil, to protect his family, to get his life back. He found himself being able to read Old Testament passages where the men were principled yet still men of the sword.

The New Testament seemed impotent to speak to him, except for these ringing words of the apostle Paul: "I don't really understand myself, for I want to do what is right, but I don't do it. Instead, I do what I hate…I am not the one doing wrong; it is sin living in me that does it." Whatever was at work in him, Michael believed it was God. Even though sometimes it felt like his flesh, and the flesh is dumb. The devil or his representatives were at work as well.

He was confused. Who was it that he was following? Whose disciple was he? He wasn't sleeping much, but a five-hour energy drink in the day and two Ambien in the night helped.

His cell phone buzzed. It was a secure phone that connected him with Jack Larsen, whose mountainous ranch's isolation made most calls impossible. He needed to talk to Jack but not yet to Jen and the kids. They might ask too many questions that he wasn't ready to answer.

"Your man is Alonzo Alvarez, Jesús' older brother. He used to be 100 percent dirty, but over the last twenty years he's gone 90 percent legal. He has fashion houses in Paris and Milan, casinos everywhere from Kiev, Budapest, and Monte Carlo to Ping Pong, Oklahoma. He is worth more than eleven billion, lives in a penthouse overlooking Central Park, and spends half his time in Europe. There are four brothers in all: Jesús, Franco, Carlos, and himself. He is known as a stone killer; he leaves no witnesses. He has killed family members.

"You are a biblical man. This guy is a cross between Herod the Great and Nero. There is no one he won't kill— women, children, dogs and cats, even the family parakeet." Jack's thorough report went on for several minutes.

"How is my family?" Michael was desperate to hear

Jen's voice.

"Jen is reading and praying a lot, spending a lot of time playing Monopoly with Corey and Janie. The kids love going outside for walks. They miss you, Michael, but you're doing the right thing. They are safe."

Michael's mind was eased. And he knew his next move: go to New York and begin the chase. "Text me his address in New York; I'll check it out."

"Okay, talk again soon." Jack hung up.

Michael flipped on the TV as he began to pack his bag. What he saw stopped him. He couldn't move as the newscaster reported the killing of Lieutenant Kenneth Bohannon of the Marion County Sheriff's Department. He had been killed in his home, and there were two suspects. Pictures of Carlos and Franco Alvarez came on screen as men wanted for questioning.

The name *Alvarez* got Michael in motion again. It was all clear, they had come to Indy to find him and Clarke, and they found Kenny and settled the score. That meant that it was highly likely that Kenny talked and had offered up him and Clarke. The whereabouts of the two men were unknown, but Michael knew the two brothers were next on his to-do list.

He called Clarke. "Listen, I know you are enraptured with the Sisters of Charity, but we have work to do." He filled him in on everything he knew.

Clarke was ready to go. "I thought you'd never ask. Come and get me, and we'll make a plan for the other brothers. Any longer here, and I would have taken a vow of chastity." Clarke was always good for an inappropriate comment.

"I should leave you where you are then; the women of the world would thank me. I'll be there in two hours. We need one more night of charity with the sisters; I'm staying with you tonight."

Michael threw his gear in the car and was off down Interstate 65. He stopped at a McDonald's and grabbed dinner for himself and Clarke. The key to effectiveness for Michael, especially when he was alone, was to avoid floating back into his now default position, the pastoral mode. The moment he succumbed, he would lose the will to finish the job. A part of him just wanted to turn the car around, go to his study, and work on a sermon.

Clarke appreciated the fast food. "I love the salt, the cheese, the carbs, the sugar and salt—my body is so happy." Michael could barely make out what he was saying through the mouthful of Big Mac.

He had to laugh at his old buddy. "I'm glad you got your fix. Now we must think." He took out a yellow pad.

"Must we? Where is the Chianti? It goes good with fries."

Clarke moved to put his feet up, but Michael motioned him over. "You'll need to raid the good sisters' Communion stash. Now get your butt over here."

He showed Clarke a diagram of his thoughts. "We need to work our way up the food chain until we kill the head, Alonzo Alvarez. We don't know where he is right now…probably in Europe. However, he should be home for Christmas. First, there is the matter of Carlos and Franco Alvarez, who killed Kenny. My source tells me that they left Indy with Jesús' body but never surfaced in New York.

"The police are going to find evidence at the crime scene and figure this out pretty quick. They will be looking for four people: you, me, and the brothers. To them, we are suspects; it doesn't matter who they get first. We'll need to change our appearance; we won't last long driving Jen's car or your car and looking the way we do."

Clarke just grinned. "Can I go as Elvis?"

For the next few hours, Michael and Clarke transformed themselves. Clarke would not look like James Bond again for a while. He dyed most of his dark hair blond, streaked it, and cut it short. His traditional khakis were replaced with royal blue jeans, a black turtleneck, and a black waist-length leather coat. He seemed to like it. "Where did you get this stuff, Michael?"

Michael studied Clarke, admiring his work. "What do you think I've been doing for four days?" His own appearance was crucial. He was on billboards and thousands of TV screens weekly and the Internet daily around the world, so this required some expertise in disguise.

He looked like a poor man's Robert Redford, but Redford in his prime, not the seventy-five-year-old cosmetically altered Redford of today. His bright blue eyes, sandy hair, square jaw, and confident look had to go. There was no way he would get through a bus station, let alone an airport. He colored his hair black and inserted dark contacts to take down the blue eyes. His hair was much shorter, almost a butch cut. His clothes were meant to look like he shopped at J. C. Penney, contrary to that what everyone knew about his clothing preference. People who knew him or had seen him would think Façonnable, Hugo Boss, and Prada, not Sears and Land's End.

Finally they looked the part; now the chase would begin.

— 17 —

The Benedictine Sisters thought it would be fun to drive a Honda Pilot for a few days. They only drove once a week to get some groceries.

Michael and Clarke looked downright at home in the blue Ford utility van heading east on Interstate 70 toward New York City. No officer would be looking for two hipsters in a conventional blue van judiciously driving the speed limit. Michael had his secure phone connection to Jack Larsen and would get updates through him on the whereabouts of Carlos and Franco. The old boys' network did work; former Navy Intelligence operators were assimilated quite naturally into law enforcement. If they weren't privy to needed information, they knew someone who could help.

The plan was to keep driving until they heard one way or another the location of the brothers. If they had no news on the brothers, there was at least the possibility that Alonzo himself might be in the city.

✷   ✷   ✷

Carlos and Franco were not in New York. They had stayed in the Atlantic City condo until they heard that the Marion County Sheriff's Department had issued a warrant for their arrest. Now they were on the move again.

✷   ✷   ✷

Revis and Puke had read the preliminary report on Bohannon's murder. A few prints were found, and they matched

Carlos and Franco. Their next problem was the most effective way to arrest the brothers and get them back to Indiana. They also wanted to question Michael and Clarke, but that was secondary, because they had done everyone a favor when they killed Jesús and Antonio. Revis didn't know if they should arrest them or congratulate them.

❋   ❋   ❋

It had taken fifteen hours, but as the dawn broke Michael could see the Empire State Building peeking above the morning mist. Clarke sat up in the back seat, emitting his normal morning cacophony of disgusting sounds and smells.

"Aw, we're here. I've got to go to the bathroom."

Michael laughed. "No kidding. I'll get off at the next exit." Soon he spotted an IHOP and parked.

Clarke was one for old, worn-out jokes. "Hey, isn't this where Obama got his foreign policy experience? The International House of Pancakes?"

Michael sighed. It used to be Clinton, then it was Bush, and now Obama. Who would be next?

Clarke couldn't resist. "Hillary, of course, she was a waitress here. She's got bigger balls than all of them combined."

Michael ordered the healthy breakfast: three turkey sausage links surrounded by scrambled egg whites, a bit runny, with dry whole-wheat toast. Any self-respecting truck driver would have scraped it into the trash.

Clarke looked at it and said, "That is the worst thing I have seen since a Chinese whore cooked me breakfast in Singapore in '97. When did you become a girl?"

Michael ignored him and chased the runny egg whites with his fork. Clarke got the double stack with bacon and soaked it in maple syrup. Clarke looked at his plate and proudly said, "This is what I call a breakfast. That thing on your plate is so weak, I'm surprised you could get a hard-on after eating like that."

Ignoring Clarke's diatribe, Michael said, "It's time to check in with Captain Jack, see if his network has an update on our boys." The restaurant was filling up and getting louder. Michael knew this would be a safe place to talk. Ambient noise is the great protector; no one can hear you talk.

"Jack, good morning. We are in NYC. Any news?" Michael was businesslike.

Even Jack Larsen thought 5:00 AM was early. "Everyone here is still in bed, including me."

Suddenly Michael realized he might be too focused. "Sorry, Jack, I should have waited a while. Can I call you back?"

Jack was emphatic. "No, I'm up now. Let me fill you in. Our associates there in the organized crime world tell me that Franco and Carlos are responsible for the Tri-State Area, especially when older brother is out of the country. They report that their trackers have Alonzo in Istanbul, and sources say he will be in Europe on business for at least three more weeks. Franco and Carlos are not at their homes and have not been seen in any of their usual haunts. There is some evidence that they have condos in Atlantic City. If they're still in the country, that's where they'd be. Jesús' body has been placed in a mortuary, and no services are scheduled at this time. He had no wife or children. I suppose they plan to bury him eventually, but now he is literally on ice. If I were you, I'd go to Atlantic City; I have some addresses of their properties. You should be able to find them."

Michael paused. "All right, no need to look for Alonzo; we'll do that. Are you still working on transportation to Europe? 'Cause when our work is done here, we'll need to make a quick exit."

"Yes, that is coming together. Check with me tomorrow. The family is fine. They miss you, but Jen basically knows the plan, and she can help the kids not wonder why you're not calling every day."

"Thanks, Jack." Michael pressed end call and said, "Jack will text me some addresses in Atlantic City. We'll go there and look for them. Let's get out of here." With that, the two strange-looking middle-aged men returned to the car. Their bland van made its way south toward Atlantic City, a town with a checkered past. It was presently a cross between Sodom and Gomorrah with a little of East St. Louis.

Two hours later; the van exited the Garden State Parkway and headed into Atlantic City. They drove toward the Boardwalk and passed some of the casinos, including Donald Trump's massive structure that had been a source of great fame and shame for the real estate kingpin. Atlantic City was a city reborn, but reborn to what? Michael wondered if such a place could have a soul. More troubling to him was what was happening to his own soul.

It was late afternoon before they spotted what looked like Carlos Alvarez driving a fire engine red Audi R8 out of the underground garage of a high-rise condominium. It was the third address that Larsen had given them. The first was a vacant lot; the second, a dilapidated house in the city's ubiquitous slums. They had only waited fifty minutes until the car roared past their van.

Larsen had provided them with the makes and models of the Alvarez family fleet of cars; the red Audi was listed. The question was, should they follow Carlos or enter their condo and look around? The car windows were smoked. Was Franco with him or watching TV in the condo?

Michael fired up the van, and they hurried to catch the Audi. They caught a glimpse of it as it entered the Trump Taj Mahal Casino underground parking structure. As the van followed, they could see Franco and Carlos exiting the car at the underground VIP entrance. The valet looked pretty excited to get behind the wheel of the high-performance Audi.

Michael pushed the button on the entry island, got his ticket, and made a left turn to find a parking spot, but not before Clarke jumped out to follow the brothers. It was immediately obvious that Carlos and Franco were not going onto the casino floor. Instead, they were ushered into the elevator that went to the hotel bar overlooking the city. Clarke followed them in the next elevator.

The bar was like Trump's hair, very confusing and a little something for everyone. The center of the very large space was the traditional bar with plenty of seats and flat screen TVs for the lonely and the alone. The windows were lined with chairs and tables for intimate groupings of two and four. The interior had the Indian drapes and mysterious alcoves that matched the casino's theme. The brothers slipped behind a curtain into a private space.

A few minutes later Michael joined Clarke at the bar. They picked out a table and took a look at the menu. Clarke made an observation. "Michael, we've never worked an op in such nice surroundings. Normally we're crawling through the mud or crammed into the back of a truck with five smelly soldiers of fortune. And I might add, you do look like Mark David Chapman on a weekend pass."

Michael smiled and said, "Just keep your eyes off the waitress, and see if our boys emerge from their boudoir." The waitress approached the table. She had great legs; to judge by the uniform, they were required for the job. Her face was hardened by life in general and encounters with customers like Clarke in particular.

She forced a smile and gave them a glance before she looked away and out to sea preparing to write. "Good evening. What would you like?"

Clarke, forgetting that his new hair and clothes made him look more like a washed-up Sid Vicious than James Bond, couldn't discipline himself to just order a drink. "Sweetie, what I'd like and what I can order are two separate things. I'll settle for a gin and tonic. When you come back, we can talk about what I want."

Michael rolled his eyes. "Ignore him; I always do. And I'll have your house Merlot." Her warm smile indicated she liked Michael; even the J. C. Penney wardrobe couldn't mask his charisma.

The bar was humming, between a lot of loud conversation, ESPN's *SportsCenter* from multiple TVs, and even a piano bar with a guy singing "Desperado"; it was Vegas without the talent. Michael was losing his patience. It had been ninety minutes, two glasses of Merlot, and far too many handfuls of party mix.

"We're not learning much. Is there anyone behind the curtain with them?" Just then the brothers emerged with four women, professional women, young, beautiful women who seemed to know how to treat two short Mexican thugs in overpriced clothes. They left the bar,

"Not exactly laying low, are they?" Clarke was the master of the obvious.

Michael mused, "They must have protection. The local police must know there is a warrant out on them, so the family must own the cops in this town. They couldn't do this in New York, because they don't own the cops there the same way. That's why they're here for now." Michael and Clarke got up to see if the brothers were leaving the hotel for the condo or if they had a different destination. It became obvious that they were staying in the hotel. They entered the elevator and went down two floors to one of the suites.

"Looks like we should call it a night," Clarke said, looking around. "Let's get a place to stay."

"Why not here? We're already parked, and we have enough cash. We won't have our special credit cards until Larsen sends them, but we're okay for the time being."

They checked in, went to the van, pulled out some luggage, and settled in for a night of strategy. Exactly how were they going to punch this ticket? It didn't seem important to do anything before lunch since Beavis and Butthead were up in their suite sleeping off their ride with the four whores of the apocalypse.

Clarke went out for a walk to ensure the red Audi had not left the valet parking section in the garage. He wanted to get the morning paper and coffee and enjoy the empty boardwalk on a brisk fall morning. He walked past the Hard Rock Café and onto the pier to contemplate how the hell he had got everyone into such a mess. A verse he had taught Michael in their collegiate days came to mind. The gist of it was "Don't be misled—you cannot mock the justice of God. You'll always reap what you sow." How often he had taught that God's grace does not nullify the natural law of sowing and reaping.

God will forgive me, Clarke rehearsed to himself, *but I must live with the consequences of my actions.* As he looked out to sea with his face set against the wind, for the first time in a very long time, Tom Clarke cried. He cried over his damaged faith, how he abused his ex-wives, the waste of his talent, his own stupidity, and his inability to change. The wind dried his tears.

Michael had just finished another failed attempt to read the Bible and have a normal conversation with God. There was nothing normal about what he had set out to do. He might be a trained killer, but he was no natural-born killer. Quentin Tarantino, the purveyor of gratuitous violence, obviously had a video game understanding of killing; real blood and gore would cause the filmmaker to puke out his guts.

He was sure that none of the blood-spattering directors in Hollywood from Peckinpah to Scorsese had any stomach for the real thing. It didn't matter to him if it was Stallone, Schwarzenegger, Bronson, or Harrelson. They made the films and put out the bloody video games and then claimed it all had nothing to do with school shootings. People railed against the NRA, but cable news, despite producing numerous programs on gun control, refused to take on their own industry, washing their hands in the blood of the victims.

Stop, stop, stop! Michael shook himself back to the here and now. He called Jack Larsen, this time waiting until 7:00 AM Mountain Time. "Hi, Jack; we found them. In fact we are in the same hotel."

He sounded upbeat to Jack. "How long before you activate?" Jack was thinking about what they would need for escape.

Michael pondered. "Could be as early as tonight, but probably no longer than three days. Still need to find the best place. Place, time, and mode are all still a bit fuzzy."

"Joey Ludwig will join you tonight as requested. He started out yesterday by car from Florida. He has some equipment you asked for; you remember how good he is at getting what a man needs."

Michael was running a finger down his to-do list. "Will he have the passports and new credit cards?"

"Yes, everything will be in order." Jack was finished talking, but Michael jumped in,

"Tell Jen it won't be much longer, couple of weeks tops and we will talk again."

"Will do."

Michael started to wonder where Clarke was. He put on his shoes and went down to the lobby. As he exited the elevator, he caught a glimpse of Beavis and Butthead, aka Carlos and Franco, entering the hotel's Starbucks. They ordered and sat down at the window bar. What Michael saw stunned him. Clarke was sitting next to them, Americano in hand, reading the paper. When he saw Michael, he smiled and returned to the funnies.

Michael ordered a latte and sat down alone at a table across the room. He watched as Clarke offered Carlos his sports section. Carlos nodded and took it. It was obvious that B & B had no idea who Clarke was. His disguise worked, but his blasé manner worked better. Michael was at the same time amused and nervous about Clarke's playfulness. He didn't want any problem in public. He noticed that Clarke was talking to them, and they were all laughing over something in the paper. A few minutes later, they left. Clarke shook their hands and said, "I'll see you later, guys." After a few more minutes, Clarke motioned to Michael, and they met on the elevator.

"What was that?" Michael's voice betrayed his surprise.

Clarke seemed proud. "The boys were very friendly after I broke the ice. They invited us to a private party tonight."

Michael laughed. "Us?"

"Yeah, me and my partner, Michael. We're gay. They thought such a friendly guy as me and my partner would enjoy a night at the corner of Sodom and Gomorrah. We provide the Sodom, they provide the Gomorrah."

Michael was aghast. "I'm appalled but impressed. Exactly how does this further our mission? I usually like to kill with my pants on." Michael couldn't stop laughing; this was a far cry from the Reverend Michael's normal pastoral duties.

Clarke got serious. "Hey, this is a great opportunity. We get close to them, and then taking them out will be easy. We can do it between hors d'oeuvres and the main course."

"Yeah, but aren't they being pretty sloppy? They haven't

stayed alive this long by being this stupid. They may be setting a trap."

"No, they are smart in some ways, but when it comes to sex, drink, and parties, these guys are prehistoric. They're thinking with their dicks. They are laying low, away from the wives and kids, and they think they're safe. They own the cops in this town and particularly in the casinos. It's a gift, Michael. Let's figure out how to use it."

Michael's mind started to naturally organize. Whether he was working on a raid on a rebel stronghold in Bosnia or an international pastors' conference, he loved strategy. He was a disciple of Jack Larsen, the maestro of a workable plan. The maestro was in the mountains of Santa Fe with Jen and the kids, but his genius was in the mind of Michael.

First one pictures the scene, who is there, what the rooms look like. It's not hard to kill; it's hard to kill without witnesses, leave behind no evidence, and get away safely. There would now be an additional team member. Joey Ludwig would be arriving before dinner. Joey had been instructed to meet Michael and Clarke at the hotel.

Michael went to the front desk and secured a brochure on the layout of the better suites in the hotel. He was pleased to find that there were only two floor plans. He knew Beavis and Butthead were in Suite 1613; that was what they told Clarke when they invited him to the party. Michael casually mentioned that he might want to take a suite because an additional party would join them for a few days. He asked which were available. None on the sixteenth floor; it was a private suite of rooms. Undeterred, he booked a suite just above them on the seventeenth floor. They would find a way to exit the scene to a staging area. That staging area would be their suite.

"How many people will be in the room?" was Michael's question to Clarke.

"Let's assume at least four whores, maybe more; you, me, and of course Beavis and Butthead." Clarke could be depended on to have a bit of lilt in his manner.

"Tommy, this is a private floor. I expect some guards to be up there, probably no more than a couple. They feel invulnerable here, even could be local off-duty rent-a-cops."

Under all the blarney and pathology, Clarke still had a brilliant mind. "You and I are the party boys, but Joey will be our surprise party favor. We will show up, and when the guards are attending to us, he will sneak in from the stairwell. We should cover any noise he makes if he needs to pick a lock."

The planning continued. They looked over the rooms. It was helpful that their suite had the same floor plan as the party site. If there were to be eight to ten partygoers and two guards, then they knew what they were dealing with. The biggest risk was that somehow they would recognize Michael from photos they had been given.

Or they might put two and two together when Michael and Clarke didn't consummate any sexual activity, because that was where they drew the line. There were always lines to be drawn in these operations. Sometimes it was at harming children or pregnant women, whatever, but a big broad red line was sex with your same-sex fellow operator. They were not going there—not that it had ever come up before.

"They'll probably pat us down when we arrive, so we won't have any weapons. Do you want to do a 'hand job' on this one?" This was Clarke's way of describing the snapping of a few necks.

Michael pondered it a moment. "The configuration is too unpredictable. It will require 'hand to hand,' and a lot can go wrong. I would rather wait until Joey gets in, and he can bring some tools with him." He stopped and waited for Clarke's feedback.

"We have all the women in there, and who knows, they

may invite some limp wrists to keep us company, but I don't think they know any. I believe they think we will be a bit of novelty, something that will liven up the party, to get their kink on."

Just then Joey called. Michael accepted the call. "Hey, boys, I'm in the parking garage, fully loaded. I have everything we need in a couple roller bags; I'll be right up."

Michael said, "Yeah, 1713. See you."

A few minutes later Joey had his feet up on the couch. "Well, boys, here we go again. Bring me up to speed."

An hour later, they had it figured out. A brash and crazy plan that had danger written all over it, but they were committed.

— 18 —

The elevators had been programmed, and only one of the six stopped on the sixteenth floor. It had its only VIP key card held firmly in a very large man's hand as he told Clarke and Michael, "Follow me, and I'll take you to the suite."

On the ride up, Michael was anticipating a pat-down and a couple of guards. The number 16 lit up with the appropriate ding. The doors opened, and the hallway was full of what looked like the Mexican Mafia. Michael counted nine heavily tattooed, jewelry-pierced men in black suits. They weren't cops or rent-a-cops; they were *Chaca* or Indian warriors, the bad boys that made the Alvarez family the most feared organization on the East Coast.

"Some party." Clarke was always ready with a quip, but he couldn't tell if they were there to protect or just to see the "fags." Either way, the plan was now in serious jeopardy. There was no way that Joey could account for all nine men. He was great, but not that great. The pat-down went as expected, though they did ask Clarke about the Sweet'N Low packets in his pocket,

"I don't do sugar" seemed believable to the thick-necked security guards. They entered the suite, where Carlos greeted them. "Tommy Boy, welcome. These are my friends, Lisa and Sally." One look at Lisa and Sally was convincing proof that their names were more likely Natasha and Nikita. Eastern European whores were beautiful and plentiful in the casino world.

Clarke took charge. "It's good to see you, Carlos. Very good taste, I must say. Meet my friend, Freddie." Michael had put on some jeans and a tight shirt; he looked better than he felt.

"Nice to meet you, Carlos. I've heard your parties are special."

"Have some drinks, enjoy the food. Here, meet my brother Franco." Carlos turned and walked away, taking Clarke with him. Michael and Franco were alone.

"Tell me, Freddie— that is your name, right, Freddie?" Michael nodded, "Why are you here in Atlantic City? Do you work together, or is this just social?"

Michael looked around the room. "Totally social. We're from Columbus, Ohio, and just wanted to get away." He was looking for the red wine; that was all the alcohol he ever consumed, and tonight in particular he would limit his intake.

It seemed Franco wanted to ask about the gay thing but just couldn't do it. "Enjoy the evening. It should get interesting later when everybody gets really hammered."

Michael smiled and moved toward the snacks, counting six men and eight women, way too many for any operational activity. He suspected the other two men were there just to enjoy; they looked like members of B & B's entourage. If he had a team on a communication link, he would have simply said, "Abort, abort mission now." He didn't have that option, so the evening would need to be played out. And there was always the Joey alternative.

As time passed, the conversations turned raunchier. Natasha and Nikita were hanging on Carlos, and two others were draped on Franco. The other four seemed to be interested in the four men who were left. They even seemed interested in some sort of scenario that included them and Michael and Clarke. Michael was retching inside. To him, the young women were the kind that his church was working to get out of the sex trafficking business in Asia. The fact that he was sitting next to a late-teens prostitute was almost more than he could bear, but he knew he must. He had learned from his mentor, Jack Larsen, that there were moments when you blocked all personal issues. You completed the mission; otherwise you died.

This was where Clarke was at his best. His brilliant and audacious mind allowed him to pull off the undoable. He looked at Carlos. "Hey, buddy, I brought you a gift."

Carlos smiled, about 50 percent operational. "What, my new friend?" His eyes were at half-mast.

Clarke pulled out the Sweet'N Low packets. "I know it says 'Sweet'N Low,' but I think you'll find this makes you sweet and high."

Carlos grew interested. "You know, I do need a pick-me-up. These girls have high expectations." Clarke and Carlos burst out in laughter.

Clarke said, "Hey, let's get Franco and go into the bedroom so we won't have to share it."

Carlos motioned to Franco. "Come with me a minute; Tommy brought us a gift."

The three of them went into the bedroom, where Clarke opened up all eight packets of the white powder. "It is some prime grade blow, boys. Enjoy." He laid it out on the coffee table. Carlos and Franco sniffed it through the straw for all they were worth.

"Have some, Tommy. Come on, join in." Clarke obliged and took a line for himself. A few minutes later, all three emerged from the bedroom looking very happy.

It only took another thirty minutes until Carlos announced, "This has been a great evening, but I'm beat. It's after midnight; let's all go home."

Clarke groaned. "Are you sure, Carlos? We were just getting started here."

Carlos looked at Franco and said, "I'm ready for bed."

Franco agreed. "Yes, everyone, good night." The women left, Michael and Clarke left, and the two friends left. The door was closed; the party was over. Michael and Clarke were taken down the elevator to the lobby.

"Well?" Michael looked at Clarke, "What happened? Did they snort it?"

Clarke smiled. "Yes they did, and by the time they are discovered tomorrow, we should be over the Atlantic sipping wine."

Michael was still curious. "Did you have any?"

Clarke winked. "Sure did, but out of a different packet. Those guys were so dumb, they'll be dead in a couple of hours."

In Joey's suitcases was a bit of strychnine. When cut properly, it would cause a slow-motion slide toward paralysis. In a few minutes neither Carlos nor Franco would be able move their arms or legs or get off the bed. They would know something was wrong. They would be alive, but paralyzed. They would begin to convulse, and the convulsions would increase in intensity and frequency until their backbones arched continually. Death would come from asphyxiation caused by paralysis of the neural pathways that controlled breathing. Their last moments would be torturous, in the knowledge that two limp-wristed boys got the best of them, but they wouldn't be able to do anything about it.

✳   ✳   ✳

Alonzo Alvarez was putting his clothes back on after his weekly exfoliation at his favorite Turkish bath. He rented the entire bath for security purposes. Something about being naked with two hairy guys in little loincloths made him feel vulnerable. Anyone could walk in and shoot him, so three of his best men locked the doors and protected him during his one-hour steam bath, massage, and exfoliating body scrub.

He enjoyed the historic baths more than the newer ones at the Four Seasons or the Hilton. He stayed at the

Four Seasons in Istanbul, even though it once had been a prison. He didn't expect to spend one more day in jail; Mexican jail was enough for one lifetime.

One of his men knocked on the dressing room door. "Mr. Alvarez, your assistant wants you to call her immediately." AA sighed and picked up his phone. He had a two-hour briefing every day, so why now? What was so urgent?

The news couldn't have been worse: Carlos and Franco found dead in their hotel suite. He fell into his chair and sat in the dressing room with a blank stare for what seemed a very long time.

Twenty minutes later, he burst from the dressing room in full stride, his guards scrambling to keep up. He slipped into the backseat of his chauffeured SUV, and it sped away up the narrow and hilly red brick streets of the old city. He started to punch his speed dial, but the three people on it were now dead; he had no brothers left. Tears ran down his face, his mind swirling with memories of Franco and Carlos, of Jesús.

The anger began to rise. He whispered to himself, "This is war, this is war, this is war." Now all he had to do was find out who did it.

He decided it was time to cash in a few chips. Captain Ray Eagan had been on the Alvarez payroll for eleven years and provided AA with important NYPD information concerning any proposed action against his business. This was especially important in the earlier years before his move toward legitimate business. He was not accustomed to actually talking to the man himself; that was much too risky.

When they were both young, they met on the street, where Alonzo ruled and Eagan walked his beat. They had reached a truce, something necessary for their mutual survival. A captain had a lot of power, and he could find out almost anything because of the networking he had to master to achieve the most coveted rank.

When Eagan answered his cell, he was surprised to hear Alonzo's voice. It was enough to get him to leave his chair and close the office door.

— 19 —

If Jen Hart had not called Sally Bohannon, Alonzo would never have found Jen and her kids. But she had made the call; she couldn't not contact Sally when she found out that Kenny had been killed.

Jack had exhorted her not to make any calls on her cell phone, because they could be traced, but to Jen it was worth the risk. She reasoned it would take a federal warrant from the Department of Homeland Security, and no thug could get that done. She was wrong; a thug could if he knew a well-connected and properly motivated captain in the NYPD.

That was why Jon Parker and Dustin McMurray were enjoying the beauty of the Sangre de Cristo Mountains as their private jet lined up for a landing at the Taos Regional Airport. The beautiful mountains' name was Spanish for the "Blood of Christ." It was early evening, and the sunset cast a red hue over the fourteen-thousand-foot summit.

They were there to conduct a bloody business, nothing that Christ would condone. Alonzo Alvarez was to have his revenge. Parker and McMurray were instructed to have no mercy; kill everyone. They would need to find the Larsen ranch, located somewhere is a five-mile-square region in the mountains outside the small town of Taos. The two assassins rented a car and began the short drive into town.

Alvarez sent two operators from outside the family because heavily tattooed thick-necked Mexicans wouldn't be able to blend into the population as nicely as the two conservatively dressed white men. They checked into a nondescript hotel and immediately experienced the thinness of that air at sixty-nine hundred feet above sea level.

Taos was for the avant-garde, a poor man's Aspen, with

an art gallery for every taste and a religion for every whim, especially for those who didn't want a god who could hold them accountable. The town exemplified the truth that if there is no orthodoxy, there can be no heresy.

For Jack Larsen, it was the most secure place he could live and satisfy his wife's need to be an artist. Situated just five miles north of Taos, it provided quiet and the *chi* Amanda Larsen claimed she needed. When Jack had retired from the Navy ten years ago, they built their dream home on the slopes. There was skiing nine months a year for Jack, hiking, hunting, reading—and of course Jack had his little own home business, providing intelligence for his former team members. Amanda kidded Jack about playing soldier, saying, "Old soldiers don't die, they become consultants."

When friends from the church or community would come by, Amanda would often apologize that Jack was in his bunker and couldn't be disturbed, and would add that he was already disturbed. She agreed to let Jack build his personal bunker lodged into the side of the hill a hundred yards from the main house. It couldn't be seen from the house or road; it was actually beyond some boulders up the hill, hidden from sight. That way she could have her studio in the main house, a place to paint, sculpt, and be alone.

Parker and McMurray knew they weren't in a John Wayne Western where everyone looking for someone started in the local saloon. They started their day at what might be considered a modern-day saloon, Elevation Coffee, a faux hipster upscale shop where people hung out in the mornings. They had pictures of Jen, Corey, and Janie on their phones, but their intel only told them that her phone call had come from the immediate region. They didn't know where she was staying or with whom.

After coffee, they went to a real estate office and found the eager sales staff more than willing to tell them about the houses in the five-mile region north of the city. They learned that some famous people lived in the area; the actress Julia Roberts had a home nearby. They also learned that most of the home sites on the slopes were five to ten acres in size, only a few were for sale, and most had been developed in the last twenty years.

Parker and McMurray said they were looking for a small ranch, and money was not an issue. The sales staff pegged them as a rich gay couple from New York looking for a Western hideaway. The next two days were devoted to spending time with Joann Thompson, a friendly and talkative agent, who knew everyone in the area. It worked like a charm. By the end of day two, after looking at fifteen properties, the assassins knew what they needed to know.

A woman and two children, a boy and a girl, were seen at Elevation Coffee and had been to some shops in town. They were friendly and were staying with a local artist, Amanda Larsen, and her retired husband. All this flowed from Joann Thompson in answer to the question, "This town seems so small. Do you notice it when someone new comes to live here?" It was just a matter of time before a real estate agent would tell everything you wanted to know about a city.

This piece of information was a good start, and it told Parker and McMurray something very important; Jen would not be out and about if she thought she was in danger. She was just a pastor's wife staying with friends while her husband was on a mission. They were confident that a retired couple trying to protect their marks would be no match for the killers.

It was 9:25 PM when they nudged their car onto the road and crested the hill in Jack Larsen's one-mile driveway. As they eased over the hill, Parker could see the lights were still on in most of the house. Both men put on ski masks. They were armed with knives, and each had a revolver. They each held a Bushmaster .223 assault rifle. They began walking toward the house. They were so confident, they walked in the open on the driveway two hundred yards from the house.

Jack Larsen knew they were there the moment they crossed the end of his driveway. Israel has such a sophisticated detection technology that it knows when a jackrabbit jumps across their border. Jack Larsen helped the Israelis install the system; why wouldn't he have it around his ranch?

When the alarm went off, Jen was doing evening prayers with Corey and Janie. Jack came to the bedroom door and said, "Come with me now, right now!"

Jen saw Jack's eyes and jumped up. "Let's go, kids." Off they went along with Amanda to Jack's bunker. Even Amanda didn't know all that Jack did in his bunker; wives never really know what dangerous men do. They walked up the path without a light, silently, in single file, holding hands; any light would reveal their location. Jack directed them to a back room in the bunker, and Jen was surprised that the bunker was so large.

The outer room had a desk, a computer, and an impressive library. Jack loved to read, and he was given to buying first editions of every kind of book. It appeared to be a room that most teachers or scholars would feel comfortable in. That was the room that Jack showed his friends and family. A second room had a bed and a flat-screen TV and was something like a motel room, except for a few electronic screens that allowed him to watch over his ranch.

The third room only Jack entered, except on a couple of occasions when Amanda had wanted to see his surveillance equipment. The room was almost wall to wall in illuminated screens. Some scanned his property, though others were cameras that were scanning hotel lobbies, public buildings, and military installations. The eleven screens showed Jack nearly all he needed to know in order to satisfy his clients.

Jen and the kids along with Amanda went into Jack's sleeping room; he went straight to the fourth hidden room. It was ten by twelve and packed with enough firepower to fight a small war. He grabbed his night-vision goggles, a knife, two Glocks, and a 12 gauge Benelli M4 shotgun. He headed out the door, handing one of the Glocks to Amanda. "If you need to, shoot to kill." He had trained her, and she was a crack shot.

Jen looked at Amanda. "Do you know how to use that?"

Amanda smiled. "You betcha, little darling. Everything will be okay; Jack is not someone you want to make mad."

Jen finally asked, "What is going on?"

Jack stopped and knelt down in front of Jen and the kids. "I'm not sure, Jen, but somehow the bad guys have found us. Don't worry, I know where they are, and there are only two of them."

Jack turned and disappeared. His legs weren't what they once were. He ran down the path, now able to see with his night vision. The two men were fifty yards from the house. Jack slipped around to the right of the house, went into a crouch at the front corner, and saw them.

McMurray was coming his way; Parker was moving to the other side of the house. McMurray was only ten feet away. Jack pulled out the knife, and when McMurray came around the corner, Jack jammed the knife deep into his throat and pulled it back with a twist. McMurray, unable to talk, let alone yell, dropped silently to the ground. Ten years was a long time, but Jack still knew his craft.

He turned to look for Parker. He knew something was askew. He saw no one in the lighted rooms and started around the outside of the house expecting to find Parker coming in his direction with the same thought: no one was home, but the lights were on.

*　*　*

Parker came around to the back of the house and slipped in through the sliding glass patio door to begin searching the rooms. Just then he heard footsteps. He turned and complained, "Where the hell you been?"

Jack called out, "Drop your weapon." Parker said nothing. He swung his gun around to pull the trigger, but before he could, the shotgun blast threw him back against the wall. He slid to the floor, leaving a red smear.

Jack was pissed. He mumbled to himself, "Don't know who they are. I only know who sent them, and how do I explain the bodies, the missing tourists, to Shorty at the sheriff's and my buddies at the Coffee Spot?" It would be a simple story: *Two men tried to rob my house. Too bad they didn't know I was armed. I'm an old Special Forces guy. I went out after them*—and there would be no more questions asked at this level of enforcement.

Jack picked up the phone and called the sheriff. Shorty and the boys drove out to the ranch. Jack told his story. Three hours later, the bodies were gone. Jack and Amanda went to bed, and Jen and the kids slept together huddled in one bed. Jack went right to sleep; no one else did.

The next morning, Jack assured Jen and the kids that everything was okay, even though he knew it was only a matter of time until Alonzo Alvarez learned of his foiled plan. He knew that whatever chance there was that Michael would not kill Alvarez was gone. When he heard of this, there would be no stopping him.

— 20 —

It had only been a few days that Michael had been back "in the life," a life of darkness, deception, and conspiracy, of plotting against your fellow man—a life of violence and death. He remembered why he'd wanted out so many years ago and how he'd sought new life in the safe confines of a theological seminary and in the arms of a new wife.

He was on the prowl again, like a well-trained animal. It was like nothing else one could feel. Life as a predator was eating at his conscience. He missed Jen desperately. Rather than pray, he repeated her name over and over. He lay in the dark in the fetal position, but he couldn't see her until the deed was done.

It had been hours since they had left Carlos and Franco to slowly die in their suite. It was about lunchtime; the bodies had been discovered and Alonzo should know by now that all his brothers were dead. He was a man of action, and that action had begun. He was probably on his way to a private airport and then would be over the Atlantic in his G650 headed to New York City.

The debate was on. Clarke and Joey were ready to hop their planned flight on Turkish Airlines 401, from JFK to Istanbul's Atatürk Airport. Michael wasn't so sure.

"Listen guys, our plane might collide with Alvarez's as he flies home to bury his three brothers. He is coming to New York. I know you think this is weird, but he is a very religious man, and family is first. That is why you have to kill him; he won't stop until he gets his revenge. But there is one thing for sure: he is going to make sure all three freaks will get a requiem mass. He needs to get them into heaven and he is willing to pay for it to happen."

Clarke was frustrated. "So what do we do? We've got

his brothers dead, but the police and Alvarez have a general description of who we are. Why would we stay here? Crazy, Michael, crazy."

Joey knew what to say: "Yeah, and look at our accommodations. We are in my pickup truck. Yes, it's big, but where do we go? Where do we hide, and then what are we going to do when and if Alvarez gets to New York?"

Clarke had an idea. "Tony Soprano, doesn't he live around here? Jersey, right. Tony will take us in, Michael; he needs some pastoral counseling with all those family problems."

As usual, Michael ignored Clarke's attempt to provide some comic relief. Also as usual, he was expected to make the decision.

"Okay, guys, let me call Jack and see what his network knows. In the meantime, let's get some lunch."

✴   ✴   ✴

It was just then that Joey's Dodge 1500 with the double cab and the secured locked bed with an arsenal on board exited the Lincoln Tunnel into New York City. A few minutes later, Michael noticed Ben's Best Kosher Deli. "Let's go there. I saw it on the Food Network, that *Diners and Dives* show; they probably take cash."

They went in, and as usual, Clarke chatted up the waitress. Joey scanned the menu, and Michael stepped outside to call Jack. He couldn't believe what Jack told him. "Let me talk to Jen. I need to talk to her." Michael tried to calm his frantic nerves.

"Michael, honey." Jen seemed calm but weepy. "We're all right, but it was horrible. We were all so scared. The kids knew it wasn't according to plan. They've been very upset. Michael, when will this all be over?" Jen's voice trailed off;

she was being quiet so the kids couldn't hear.

"Jen, I'm so sorry." He knew she could feel the pain in his voice. "I'm working on it; it won't be long. This whole thing will be over before my sabbatical ends, and then we will have some peace. I love you. Tell the kids that I love them. I am out here doing the right thing to solve the problem, okay? Will you tell them that?" He waited for the words he needed to hear.

"Yes, Michael. You're my protector, and I trust you completely." Jen's voice had an ought-to sound. She knew she had to hang in with Michael.

He had said enough to reassure her. He had only to wrap up this conversation. "I promise you, Jen, we will never have to deal with these people again."

Jen couldn't hold back: "Michael, how are we ever going to be normal again? How are you going to be able to be a pastor again? I'm totally confused. I don't know how to pray, 'Oh Lord, make my husband a great killer. May his aim be straight, may his hands be quick, and may he not hesitate in the moment he is required to take a life'?"

Michael listened quietly and said, "Yes, pray for that. That would be good."

✻   ✻   ✻

Jen handed the phone back to Jack and went to her room to cry, to pray, to doubt, to believe, and everything else that came to mind for her to do. Jack put the phone back up to his ear, not knowing what he would hear.

Michael spoke first: "Thanks, Jack. You saved my family. I will never be able to pay you back."

Jack was all business. "Listen, I've got it here. You get it done there. News on the network is that Alvarez will return to New York to bury his brothers. But he had a big meeting in Istanbul, which he has delayed for a week. I would advise you to proceed to Istanbul. You have travel plans, all the papers, and the reservations for you are all set up. You will arouse less suspicion by following the schedule. That will give you time there to prepare for his return."

Twenty hours later, Turkish Air Flight 401 touched down in Istanbul. From the air, the ancient city once named Constantinople looked as inviting as San Francisco on a beautiful day. From three thousand feet you could see where Europe touched Asia, the rolling hills surrounded by the glistening water that also ran through it. This crossroads between East and West had a bloody history. One could see why: ships were lined up waiting to go up the Bosphorus passage that allowed them to pass from Europe to Asia, from the Sea of Marmara to the Black Sea. The armies of the world had always sought to control this passageway. Whoever held the Bosphorus held this strategic outpost.

Once the Eastern seat of the Holy Catholic Church, the city now had a skyline dominated by the minarets of the ubiquitous mosques. The red-roofed homes nestled on the hills were a feast for the eyes. The beauty stirred a prayer in Michael. He felt like a tourist. He couldn't wait to get out and see the great religious history, places he had heard of, battles he had studied—even a trip to Nicaea might be in the offing, depending on how long Alvarez stayed in New York.

Ten hours in economy class had its way of making a person anxious to get off a plane. The three "tourists" had limited funds, plus economy-class passengers attracted less attention. Michael's mind went clear when he glanced at his passport and saw the name Randall Knutson. Would it work when the transit agent slid it through his scanner? He knew by now a national or even an international dragnet would be out for him and his two companions. For that reason they had checked in separately at JFK and traveled as strangers. They were to meet the next day at lunchtime in Sultan Ahmet Square, right in the middle of the tourist section of the old city.

＊　＊　＊

Michael felt a bit more relaxed after passing through Customs as Randall Knutson. Larsen always did good work; his information was always right, his network expert. If Jack's reports were accurate, they would need to wait at least a week for Alvarez to return for his important meetings with his distributors from the Baltic States.

It wasn't often that an internationally feared crime boss held meetings with his network of fashion designers in central Asia. But then Alonzo Alvarez was an extraordinary man. His network was conducting a manhunt; even Detectives Revis and Johnson from Indianapolis were looking for Michael and Clarke. Michael wasn't looking for anyone. He was a man in waiting, hiding in plain sight, a strange place for a natural predator.

The taxi dropped him in front of the Citadel Hotel, a reasonably nice Art Deco place with some good views. It had wireless Internet and a nice bar and restaurant. It was on the edge of the old city a few blocks from the Blue Mosque. It was also a few blocks from Alvarez's favorite haunt, a suite at the Four Seasons. Michael wanted to be able to walk; this was another way to disappear into the tourist crowds.

He felt safe in the hotel. Authorities would not be searching for him or his companions. There was no reason to look for them in Turkey; certainly Alvarez wouldn't guess it. No one would suspect that the hunted would become the hunter.

Clarke and Ludwig checked into their respective hotels; both had too much downtime. Istanbul had too many belly dancers and bathhouses for Michael not to worry, but three Westerners together in one hotel would have been noticed.

After a shower and a two-hour nap, Michael forced himself out of bed in order to set his body clock. It was time to get out and walk. He still had to keep himself awake for several hours. He had traveled much of the world during his operational days, but he was usually in a remote location or crammed into a helicopter with ten other guys. Part of getting the job done was not to be seen, and when you were prowling about in the middle of the night in order to execute orders and rid the world of bad guys, you didn't see much.

Church history was a required course in seminary. Michael liked it so much, he took four semesters instead of the two required. He knew a bit about Eastern Orthodoxy, which still existed with some power in Turkey. For nearly a thousand years, Constantinople had been the center of Christendom. How the grandeur of the Christian Constantinople became Islamic Istanbul was a bloody struggle about power and religion.

One of the first things that Michael wanted to see was the fifth century church, Hagia Sophia. It was once the symbol of Christian power, an architectural miracle in the fifth century. As Michael approached it, he saw the three minarets that now stood as a buttress to the building and a sign of the transition of power over the centuries. He wondered, as he looked up at the Arabic medallions that adorned the great inner dome of the church, how did a 95 percent Christian world become a 95 percent Islamic world?

Sociologists generally agreed that it took a nation 250 years to transition from top to bottom from a Christian nation to an Islamic nation. Constantine the Great moved the capital of the Roman Empire to this plot of land in AD 334, a city that once was ruled by Alexander the Great. Constantine had called the first church council at Nicaea, a present-day suburb of Istanbul renamed Iznik. It had seen fourteen centuries of wars, of back and forth, the Crusades, the Ottoman Empire, the Great War, and finally the Turks in 1924 had made it a secular empire. Michael, like any Christian pastor, wondered, *What went wrong here?*

He was hungry. He would come back to the church again, but for now he had to eat. He decided to walk the Hippodrome through its elongated gardens on his way to restaurant row. It was hard to believe that all that was left of a stadium that seated 100,000 were two columns: the Egyptian Obelisk from 1500 BC, covered with hieroglyphics, and the Serpentine Column from around the tenth century AD.

The sun was setting, and a subtle glow lay over the city. The beauty of the day was yielding to the artificially luminous night. Michael found his way to a kebab house. He grabbed some pita bread, hummus, and hot tea. He sat down on a stool facing the street while he waited on his chicken kebab. The music was playing loud, as it always seemed to in such places. Usually it was a Middle Eastern form of music, a woman modulating her voice very fast, a cowboy yippie-ki-yay with hummus on it. It had to, in some awful way, alter the brain waves of the owner, but maybe he just couldn't hear it anymore.

He tried to read a copy of the *International Herald Tribune*, but he was beginning to see double. He did notice two men sitting at a table outside on the sidewalk who seemed to be watching him. They looked like other Turkish men, with dark hair and eyes and dressed in nondescript slacks, shirt, and jackets to protect them from the night air. Michael read a little of the Gospel of John on his phone, where he had a 2700-page study Bible. Jesus' words jumped off the page,

"The thief comes only to steal and kill and destroy; I came that they may have life, and have it abundantly."

Michael couldn't help but think that he was more like the thief than like his Lord and leader. If other people today would criticize his hero Dietrich Bonhoeffer for cooperating with a plot to kill Hitler, certainly his parishioners would be hard on him for killing bad guys rather than loving them into the kingdom. But then his plan was that those other people would never know. He couldn't say that he and his family were experiencing the "abundant life." The very thought of Jen, Corey, and Janie having their lives threatened, the fact that Alvarez had taken the gloves off, was enough to keep Michael on task.

He stood and stretched. Slowly, but with a watchful eye, he stepped onto the street and began to walk in the direction of his hotel. The street was crowded with early evening patrons out for dinner and shopping. He noticed the same two men about seventy-five feet back as he moved along the busy street behind the Blue Mosque.

Michael decided not to lead the two men to his hotel. He started downhill into the winding cobblestone side streets. He took a detour, and when he turned the second time, they were gone. He couldn't tell whether it was his fuzzy, sleepless brain that imagined their sinister intention or whether they were really good trackers and would pick him up later.

He turned once more, this time toward the Citadel Hotel. Then he noticed three men walking behind him and loudly talking. They were fifty feet away but gaining on him; he thought it was a possible handoff crew. He walked past his hotel, and the three men went in. It seemed their reason for following him was they were staying in the same hotel. Michael turned around and went back to the hotel. He returned to his room and laid his head down on the pillow.

"I guess no one is looking for me yet, at least here."

— 21 —

It was nearly 11:30 when Clarke and Joey joined Michael at the Beyazit Gate entrance to the Grand Bazaar. Michael's theory was the more tourists, the more you blend in. They picked a nice little restaurant a few yards away from the gate that specialized in the tourist trade. Michael liked it because it wasn't playing any music; he hated what Clarke called tabouli music. They waited a couple of minutes and finally were seated.

"Good to see you guys and know you survived twenty-four hours without me." He laughed as Clarke and Joey smiled. Then he got serious. "Did you notice anyone or anything that caught your eye?"

Clarke looked at Michael with a twinkle. "Yeah, I thought her belly would never stop moving. I couldn't believe anyone could do that with their body; it was amazing. She could have danced all night, but I interrupted her a few times so she could earn her tips." He paused for effect. "Apart from that and the Turkish bath yesterday afternoon, not a thing." Clarke took a swig of beer.

Michael looked at Joey. "So what about you? Different hotel, I'm afraid to ask, but what happened with you?"

Joey seemed nonplussed. "I went to the same Turkish bath with Tommy Boy. Those dudes that work on you, they were born with hair shirts. They beat the hell out of us, but it was a good pain. It's like being mauled by a grizzly. You need to go, Michael. You will never feel better than after having been abused."

Clarke reminded Michael of Joe Walsh, the lead guitarist for the Eagles. He was kind of crazy but great at what he did. Clarke was about to have a serious moment. He was still brilliant, even when he was sober.

"Michael, what is the plan? We can't just sit around here and wait. What action can we take? Let's do something, get inventive like we did in Atlantic City."

Michael had spoken that morning with Jack and had some information. "I am not sure yet, but I think the right device under a limo could send him flying in several directions." He took out a sheet of notepaper. "Alvarez is fond of limousines. Wherever he goes, he stays in the best hotels, eats the best food, uses the best cars, and hires the best whores. It seems to be a family trait with the women. Like the Eagles sing in 'Life in the Fast Lane,' 'They threw outrageous parties, they paid heavenly bills.' We find the limo service cars, do a little research, and boom, Alonzo meets his maker."

Joey nodded. "I like it—explosives, no shootouts; we could be watching from a distance. Enjoy it with a sip of wine."

Michael folded the paper and put it back in his pocket. "All right, Joey, you figure out what we need to ignite the limo. Tom, you do the limousine research. I will keep talking with Jack and find out how long we have until Alonzo returns."

It was after 2:00 PM when they went their separate ways with plans to meet again the next evening for drinks at the Four Seasons. It was a bit of a gamble, but they wanted to see the layout.

❋　❋　❋

It had been just over a week and Puke was assessing the body count. Revis had his feet on his desk, hands clasped behind his head, with eyes closed, listening.

"Jesús Alvarez is dead, and so is his pal Antonio. Add to that Kenny Bohannon, and now according to this report,

Jesús' two brothers, Carlos and Franco, poisoned in Atlantic City at Trump's Casino. Someone is very effective, and I think we have a suspicion who that someone is."

Revis sat back up in a normal position. "He walks like a pastor, he talks like a pastor, but he is a killer "

"We have no trace of him or Clarke, any of them for over a week now."

Revis was more curious than puzzled. "Why would he do it? He is on a sabbatical for a month, they are off into the mountains, there is no proof."

Puke kept reading the report: "The witnesses say there were two men at the party, but the descriptions are not anything like Hart and Clarke. They were the same approximate age and height, but hair color and clothes do not fit their type. They also were partying with a group of professional ladies. Doesn't sound like Hart, though it does sound like Clarke. They paid for their room in cash, and they arranged for a third party one night. If it was Hart and Clarke, they slipped away."

Revis pondered for a minute. "How did they get away? What do the hotel's surveillance tapes show?"

Puke pulled out the printouts. "They show three men with hats and shadowed faces walking through the garage onto the street and out of view. If it was them, they added a third, which jives with the hotel bill."

Revis stood and stretched. "We've got a lot of suspicion and a hell of a circumstantial case against Hart and Clarke. So far, however, I must admit they are dispensing the justice of angels. They have been able to do more to end crime in Indianapolis and New York City than the police."

Puke laid down the file. "We'll just need to wait until they resurface. When they do, we'll be able to interview them, unless the Alvarez crew kills them. But I think I'd put my money on the good reverend."

— 22 —

Three white hearses carrying the bodies of Jesús, Carlos, and Franco Alvarez followed by four white limousines slowly pulled up in front of St. Patrick's on Madison and Fifth Avenue. The Gothic cathedral stood in all its splendor as a bulwark against the madness of modern life. And nothing could be madder than the duplicitous Catholicism practiced by Alonzo Alvarez and his family. They wanted forgiveness for their sins and revenge against their enemies.

This was clearly in focus as the grieving kingpin of the financial empire that was Alvarez Inc. screamed into his phone, chiding his search team for its failure to find another conflicted religious man, the Reverend Michael Hart. He was convinced that he was now the hunted, but he wanted to hunt too. He was accustomed to spreading his own brand of fear and mayhem; he didn't like the fear that now visited his gut. As the car came to a stop, he started to think about the two trailing limousines carrying the two grieving widows of Franco and Carlos and their seven children. He alone felt the pain deeply for baby brother Jesús, the one he had actually raised.

The service was conducted by a local priest who ministered in the New York diocese, and of course Alvarez made sure all his employees, from his fashion houses to his whorehouses, to the cops he owned and the chain of convenience store operators he managed, were all in attendance. The public would have to wait a couple of hours to get their TV dinners, chips, and snacks. During the high requiem mass there were many tears and prayers. The women and children cried, but none more than Alonzo himself. He wept uncontrollably because of the wrong he had done his mother. Because of him, three of her sons were dead.

He was grateful she wasn't there to suffer through it herself.

He swore on the Virgin Mother that people would pay. Millions would burn in Hell for rejecting the Blessed Mother's Son, and now many would suffer for hurting his mother's sons. Alonzo didn't seem to connect his own family's role in their deaths. His theology was simple: absolution through the church and retribution through him.

It came time for a family tribute. Alonzo Alvarez would now make a speech, something he usually reserved for his explosions of controlled rage and profanity-laced tirades. He slowly ascended the steep stairs of the chancel with a note sheet in hand.

"Today is a solemn day for the Alvarez family. My three precious brothers lay before you, all dead by the evil hand of hatred. Franco, forty-one; Carlos, thirty-seven; and Jesús, thirty-one, all struck down in the prime of life, and why? Maybe Father José will be able to help us with the why, but I can promise you their passing does not go unnoticed by their elder brother. I will see to it that justice is done. I will bring all my power and fortune to bear on this group of men who have taken from us what can never be replaced. I promise you, Rose and Maria, that your husbands have not died in vain.

"Jesus said, 'Of the one to whom much is given, much is required.' I have been given much, and now I will require the men responsible for this to receive sure justice administered by my hand."

With that, Alonzo Alvarez descended the stone stairs and returned to his seat. It didn't bother him that he had promised to take matters into his own hands in front of more than ten police officials; after all, they were on his payroll. As the priest led the caskets in the recessional, Alvarez took his Carmen's hand and followed them to the graveside service, which would not end for another ninety minutes. His heavily tattooed hand wrapped around her delicate, bejeweled fingers reminded one of a Guns N' Roses dress-up event.

By 6:30, Alvarez was surrounded by his search team as they combed the globe looking for Michael Hart or Tom Clarke. The men had vanished since leaving the Trump in Atlantic City; they were not in Indiana, and they were not in New York or the Tri-State Area.

Alvarez was fuming as he studied the room. "I've given you the best equipment and resources money can buy. Now, dammit, I want results!" Captain Eagan had searched the FBI, NYPD, and Interpol databases. He had even tried Naval Intelligence, but couldn't get it done. The local pimps, hoods, drug dealers, restaurateurs, and convenience store operators were put on alert with five-hundred-dollar rewards for relevant tips.

The captain had nerve enough to speak. "AA, they could have left the country. If I were you, I would check the cities that you frequent, where you plan to be soon. They are aggressive; they could be looking for you."

Everyone in the room could tell that Alvarez was considering Eagan's words. "If he is looking for me, he will gag on my balls. He's never tasted anyone like me. He better hope he dies before I get my hands on him; it will take me three days to kill him." He seemed to feel better about it now.

＊　＊　＊

The next few hours for the Alvarez family were a strange mix of sobbing, dancing, praying, drinking, outbursts of anger, and some ill-advised explosions of sex around the family compound between cousins, shirttail relatives, waitresses, busboys, and anyone else who could get away with it before dawn.

Most of the partakers in the fleshpots of the night struggled with puffy faces and blurry eyes to get to the required morning family mass previously arranged by Alonzo. It was to be held at AA's penthouse, and no one would dare miss. The entire mourning family, it seemed, had missed none of the sinful activities of the night before: "sexual immorality, impurity, lustful pleasures, idolatry, sorcery, hostility, quarreling, jealousy, outbursts of anger, selfish ambition, dissension, division, envy, drunkenness, wild parties and other sins like these. Let me say again, as I have before, that anyone living that sort of life will not inherit the Kingdom of God."[1] They would keep the priest busy until nearly lunch in his confessional.

Alvarez practiced an abusive user mentality of Christ's sacrifice for his sin, he believed in forgiveness without repentance, confession without remorse, a new start without change. If ever a man knew how to cheapen Christ's sacrifice and His grace, it was Alonzo Alvarez. His duplicitous life was largely a product of his ignorance of the Bible and even the Catholic Church's teaching. He didn't seem himself much different than the great football coach, Vince Lombardi, who was an altar boy each morning and a cursing, angry, hard drinking, spitting mad football coach by day.

The Catholic Church had a long tradition of lusty men of the world getting absolved of their sins on Sunday so they could go back and do the same thing over and over again week after week. Then they'd obtain a priestly pass to heaven in exchange for a nice donation. The mythological Michael Corleone of *Godfather* fame was working his legacy and eternal dwelling in *Godfather III* by making large donations to the church. Alvarez was continuing in what he thought the great men of the world had done.

❋   ❋   ❋

[1] *Galatians 5:19–21, New Living Translation*

Whatever corrupted ideas Alonzo Alvarez had about his redemption, his struggle for it could not have been any greater than the Reverend Michael Hart's.

Michael once again spent a morning wandering the streets of the ancient center of the once imperial Catholic Church. He was theologically astute and well-versed in both Scripture and theology. His tormenter was truth. As he had pointed out many a time in sermons, Jesus said, "If you continue in my word, you are truly my disciples; and you will know the truth, and the truth will make you free." He had jokingly pointed out some alternative readings, "The truth will set you free, but first it will make you miserable." Another favorite was "You shall know the truth, and the truth will make you flee." At this point, he both was miserable and wanted to flee. He wanted to get out and return to normal, but he was trapped. Trapped like a cancer patient is trapped in his or her body, unable to get rid of the problem without eliminating the body. So he slipped his tourist map into his back pocket and stepped off the curb heading for his rendezvous at the Four Seasons Hotel.

It was just after 6:00 PM when Michael spotted Clarke and Joey seated in the piano bar. As one might expect in one of the finest hotels in Europe, the walls were a sunny yellow, the furnishings were Art Deco, and all the windows were beautifully appointed and rounded at the top, allowing one to step out onto the patio just in the shadow of the Hagia Sophia. The sun was down, and the blue lights made for a gorgeous night as the mosque shown in all its glory.

"Let's go out on the patio. I'd like to enjoy the night." Michael was emphatic.

Clarke rolled his eyes. "All right, Mikey is missing Jen. Let's go out on the patio and hold his hand. Doesn't matter that it can't be more than fifty out there." Joey and Clarke grabbed their coats and joined him.

Michael leaned back and lifted the Turkish Merlot to

his lips. "I'm sure Jesus made better wine than this, and it didn't cost twenty bucks a glass." Another taste slipped down his gullet; Michael was in a reflective mood. "What would Jesus do if He were in my shoes, boys?"

Joey laughed and looked at Clarke. "Is he always this philosophical with wine? What's next, the Lord's Prayer?"

Clarke began to chuckle. "Yeah, you know that Lord's Prayer, don't you, Joey? 'Now I lay me down to sleep, I pray the Lord my soul to keep.'"

Joey wasn't that good with theology; he made things blow up. He was reduced to a smirk.

Michael went on, "I've mulled it over, guys. How can we get out of this, how can we avoid this war? I think we are stuck; the only way out is our plan. I have entertained the pacifist way, just asking God to protect us, but God Himself was a warrior. He didn't go that route in the Old Testament. I don't believe God changes. He is the same; fighting is part of who He is. I just don't know what it will do to me, to Jen, to the kids, and to my relationship to God."

Clarke understood Michael's angst, but his conscience had been seared by years of being out of it spiritually. He couldn't even join the discussion. Joey's mind wandered back to south Florida and Cheryl's hot oiled body slithering up and down his torso. He was feeling good.

The waiter brought out a Black Sea specialty, *hamsi pilav*, a pungent mixture of anchovies and rice. This was followed with *yalanci yaprak dolmasi*, vine leaves stuffed with mussel and rice. The smell itself was enough to change the subject.

Clarke got serious, which was rare, so Michael and Joey sat up in their chairs. "It looks from basic surveillance as if the hotel layout is simple. There are several exits, but only one that would service limos, and there are several spots from which we can enjoy the proceedings. The deluxe suites have no special exits; the patrons must all pass through normal doors. So none of the Princess Diana stuff of trying to leave via a servant's entrance to avoid the paparazzi; he would get picked up out front.

"They normally use Alexi Auto Service. Alonzo really likes the special armored SUV made by BMW, a combination of bulk, speed, and the emblem that says money. He is worth billions, and he likes for people to know it. He can't seem to get over being raised in the Mexico City dump."

Michael nodded. "Joey, have you found the resources we will need?"

Joey was still a bit choked up by his first bite of mussel and rice. "Yeah, the man was at the address Frank gave us. He had everything I needed. I will only be able to test its potency in very small amounts. I will test it for sure; I don't want to be like the amateur bomb maker on the Israeli assassination team in the film *Munich*. He would use too much and then in the next hit, too little. I intend it to have just the right kind of boom."

Michael seemed satisfied and started summing up. "Okay, we probably have three days until our person of interest returns for his big meeting here in the hotel. He will be using some of the meeting rooms on the first floor. His people will fill up at least 50 percent of this place, and security will be fifty or more armed personnel. As far as I know, he doesn't own this hotel, but he could have his people in place already. Have you noticed any people around you that you are seeing repeatedly?"

He could tell that neither Joey nor Clarke had thought much about whether they were being watched.

❋   ❋   ❋

From across the Four Seasons' well-marbled lobby the three Americans leaving didn't seem too abnormal, but Alonzo's personal concierge, Elif Bata, made a note anyway. Michael, Joey, and Clarke couldn't have been more than fifty yards down the street when a text popped up on Alonzo's personal assistant's phone, "three Americans who are not hotel guests here for dinner."

The assistant replied, "Get description and we will have our people there check it out." Unbeknownst to Michael and company, they had been noticed.

Fifteen minutes later, even though it was 10:15 PM, a black Mercedes pulled up to the hotel, and two men in the obligatory black leather jackets and jeans hopped out and spent over an hour interviewing Elif and other hotel personnel, especially the maître d' and the American men's waiter. "What did they talk about? What did they order? How much did they eat and what did they drink? Did they say where they were staying?" The most important information was their age and state of fitness and whether they seemed like tourists who would volunteer facts about themselves or were more circumspect.

At 1:15 AM Istanbul time, 6:15 PM in New York, Alonzo had the report in front of him as he prepared to dine with his leadership team. The report read,

"The three men fit the description of the three men in Atlantic City who our security detail saw in the hallway outside of Franco's and Carlos's hotel suite. Their demeanor and discussion in the hotel restaurant didn't seem to characterize them as tourists. They seemed to be interested in the layout of the hotel and were actually looking at the floor plan in the brochure. Their brazen behavior of being at the hotel and showing themselves indicates the same aggressive conduct in their pursuing Carlos and Franco in Atlantic City. We have conducted a citywide search of hotel records and we have activated our network of informants and personnel. We would expect that very soon we will know where these men are staying. In the meantime, it is reasonable to assume that they are planning an attack and that attack will center around your plans to stay at the Four Seasons."

Alonzo laid down the report and smiled. "I like these boys. They have very large balls. Too bad they will gag on them. I don't return to Istanbul for three more days; they should be dead by then. No, wait. I want to see them die. Let me know when you have them, and keep them alive until I get there. I want to be there when they get their skin peeled, when we cut off their dicks, when we serve them their own balls." Alonzo felt better already. His personal assistant sent a short text that conveyed what Alonzo wanted.

It didn't take long. By 7:00 AM Alonzo's men knew where Michael Hart was staying. An American staying alone in the Citadel Hotel is easy to spot, especially when you have a five-hundred-dollar incentive to energize your memory, sometimes to stimulate your imagination. But in this case, a desk clerk knew Michael's face.

❋   ❋   ❋

Having stayed in the Citadel for three nights, Michael was already familiar with the normal noises and routines of the hotel. By 7:00 he had already done his hundred push-ups and sit-ups and had his twenty minutes reading Scripture and making his own coffee. He was just preparing to sit down for some reflection time before heading down to the restaurant for breakfast.

He heard some shuffling outside his door on the tile hallway floor and knew at once what it was. He bolted to his suitcase, pulled out his Glock, screwed on the silencer, and took a position on the other side of the bed. Suddenly the door blew into the room, splintering the chair where he had been seated. The first hooded man through the door had his automatic rifle cocked and ready. Michael shot him in the neck, and blood sprayed from his carotid artery. The second shooter dived onto the floor and was on the opposite side of the bed from Michael. Michael had already moved as the gunman slid along the floor and shot him point blank in the forehead. Michael rolled to his feet looking for a third, a fourth shooter, but there was nobody. They had only sent two.

Michael sat down on the bed to try and figure out what to do. He called Clarke. "You and Joey get over here now. I've got two dead shooters in my room. We need to get them out of here or leave the country quick."

Clarke said, "Yelp," and ended the call. Ninety minutes later, the work was done. Both shooters were bagged and in the back of a rented van and off to the City's Refuse Center via special courier. The courier service didn't know their payload, but within thirty minutes two souls would be disposed of, not to be heard from again.

Michael, AKA Randall Knutson, reported his room broken into; the room would need a new door. Mr. Knutson wanted a new hotel, so he checked out. Joey and Clarke would need to move as well; they started looking for a hideout.

Jack Larsen's network found them a small farmhouse outside Iznik, a lakeside community about an hour outside Istanbul. Its ancient name was Nicaea, famous for the very first worldwide church council called by Constantine in AD 325. Three hundred bishops convened a meeting in the emperor's Senatus Palace, whose ruins now lay at the bottom of Lake Iznik. The council began to sort out the nature of Christ and the date of Easter and wrote the now famous Nicene Creed. It took the bishops a month to knock out the creed.

Michael was the only occupant of the car who had knowledge of the region's history, but didn't take time to mention it. He did think it was odd that he was rethinking who Christ was. He, however, was keeping his own counsel. The GPS got them into the general vicinity of the red roofed home sitting at the end of a lane. It was dark, but a retired colonel in the Turkish Army was there to greet them. The one thing that Special Operations alumni had worldwide was a brotherhood, old soldiers loyal to one another based on respect—a Fifth Column, so to speak, who were willing to reach across national loyalties so long as they were not required to betray their own country. The nameless man in his late fifties never spoke a word. He handed them the key and drove away.

Michael knew their time was limited. They had a car from the same resource that had furnished Joey with the explosives. They had to stop and get provisions at a supermarket while still in Istanbul; they had been seen, and it was only a matter of time until Alonzo's network would find them. The question was *Will they be able to find us before we are able to kill him?* It had become apparent that Alvarez owned as many police and governmental officials in major cities of Central and Eastern Europe as he did in NYC. If you fed the corrupt system enough cash, it racked up points like a pinball machine.

Around the crackling fire the three fugitives were crafting plan B, or was it C? Clarke was his usual cynical self. "I suppose this means we can't sneak into the open bar at Alonzo's party and feast on some of the female flesh that will be served as hors d'oeuvres." Both Joey and Michael ignored him.

Joey seemed to be fixated on the problems of blowing up Alonzo without blowing up everyone. "I think it will be tough now. They will be looking for something, and I don't think they will trust anything, especially their rented transportation. I think we will need to take it away from the hotel. It will require an on-the-move, more spontaneous hit." Joey leaned back and sipped his espresso.

Michael frowned. "I don't like our chances tailing them in our own car and then attacking a convoy of highly trained guards with good weapons and armored vehicles. We need him in a low security environment where we are not all moving sixty miles an hour."

Clarke suggested, "I don't think he will eat out during the conference; he is taking care of everyone on site. The Four Seasons has the level of service and cuisine that will keep them safely in the hotel."

Michael agreed with a nod. "Listen, Joey, I think we should stick to the original plan. Find out which SUV will be his, then rig it, he will go boom, and we will go home. That means when he returns, we need to ID the arrival car and trace it to its source. They normally keep the same fleet right at the hotel guarded 24/7."

Clarke seemed relieved. "Very good, then, boys. Let's have dinner." He got up to start the stove, Joey to open up the pasta and start the bread, and Michael to call Jack and see when Alonzo might be returning.

"Hi, Jack, how is everything there?" Michael and Jack had gotten into a normal routine: check in and talk long enough to cover relevant news, but not long enough for scanners to pick up their discussion.

Jack had some questions: "How do you want to get out of there, after you reach your goal? You will need quick extraction, right?"

Michael wasn't sure about details. "I think we will need a private plane to get us to Western Europe—Paris, Berlin, London…then we can figure it out from there."

Jack listened and then had an idea. "Our network does have access to private aircraft. We'll find a suitable time and airport for your trip, destination to be determined. Does that sound okay?"

"Yes. If you trust them, then I trust them."

Jack responded, "You'll be okay. Listen, I expect from our sources in NYC that AA will be back in Istanbul on Wednesday. That gives you two more days. You will need to get me a time of day for extraction. When you know, contact me." Michael signed off without mentioning Jen or the kids; it was just too painful. If there'd been any bad news, Jack would have told him.

✳   ✳   ✳

It was a little after noon when Alonzo Alvarez's Gulfstream G650 landed at Istanbul's Atatürk Airport. The convoy of SUVs ferried Alonzo and his entourage of fourteen to the Four Seasons. There had been enough time for a disguised Joey Ludwig to greet the three SUVs through his telephoto scope. All three SUVs were the same weight and construction, each outfitted with special security features. A bomb would need to provide enough lift and percussion to undo those features. It would have to pierce the armor, lift the car at least ten feet off the ground, and have a secondary thrust to blow it apart.

Joey sat on the patio of a café a hundred yards away, looking like a tourist with his two-week growth of beard, jeans, T-shirt, and wide-brimmed straw hat. The sandals with the brown socks were the coup de grâce—very European. Joey was more interested in where the cars would be parked and who took responsibility for them than in the bizarre characters who piled out of them. If you wanted to see new money spent badly, all you had to do was catalogue the Alvarez posse: too many tattoos, bad bling, tight-fitting leather pants with bellies and bottoms bulging and spilling over, and the sunglasses, expensive and gaudy, covering the bad plastic surgery. The women's mentor seemed to be Joan Rivers; the men's, the second coming of the overweight and puffy Steven Seagal.

The drivers sped away, but to Joey's delight only a short block away, where they took the entrance to an underground garage. A few minutes later, all three drivers walked back up to the hotel. It seemed no one stayed with the cars.

Joey had to know. He began walking toward the garage—down the hill and past the hotel—with his tourist map hanging from his pocket for effect. The Four Seasons was not the kind of place where guards stood out front, so no one paid any attention to him as he got closer to his goal. The pedestrian entrance to the car park was open, so Joey wandered in like he was looking for his own car.

There they were, all three SUVs parked side by side on the first level. They were unattended, but Joey saw the three cameras, one trained on each of the BMWs. These were newly installed cameras, state of the art, and Joey had no illusions about who was on the other end of the line. It was Alvarez's men, on round-the-clock shifts, just fifty yards away. They had to be on high alert, knowing that Joey and company were in the region. In fact, Joey thought this might be a ruse to draw them in by providing an apparent easy opening for any assailants.

Joey did not approach the cars but turned, looking in all directions and acting lost, and exited the garage. He headed away from the hotel and moved up past Hagia Sophia to sit on one of the hundreds of benches facing the church. He wondered how they might do this and, crucially, how they could get away undetected. It would be an hour yet before he would meet with Clarke and Michael, who had decided to have a coffee and talk alternatives.

— 23 —

When the car pulled up, Joey hopped in, anxious to give his assessment.

"The problem with the cars is they are surveilled 24/7 electronically by his men. The second challenge is which one will be Alvarez's car of choice; they may randomly rotate his ride for safety. A third issue is how many people we want to kill needlessly. They may be garish and ugly, but must we blow them all up?"

Michael laughed. "Sounds like we have a moral dilemma wrapped in the skin of a problem. Should we abandon the entire project?"

He never was serious when he used that sarcastic tone, so Joey was confident. "If I can find a way to wire a car, everyone in that car will be a goner. The challenge is to know when to wire it and which one to wire. Otherwise too many bad things can happen." Joey leaned back; he'd had his say.

Clarke again seemed unusually serious. "I think we are going to have to get up close. It's more effective and more humane. I would recommend exploring that possibility. He'll be here for two full days of meetings starting tomorrow. The only other possibility is a shot from a distance, but unless you can get him on the patio at night and get Michael on top of Hagia Sophia with a scope, how could it possibly be done? I'm for getting rid of the guy, but I am not willing to go stupid and get killed or captured in the process."

Suddenly it all came together in Michael's mind. "I think I know what our strategy should be. Let's work on the three fronts of our expertise. Tommy, you are all things trickery; Joey, you blow things up, and I am the shooter.

Let's work all three plans and see which one seems most right, see what opportunities present themselves. Joey, you wire the cars. Tom, you try and figure how we might get into Alvarez's hotel suite for some face time, and I will work on how to take a shot onto the balcony or the main gathering areas. Each of us work on a plan today, and tonight after dinner, each of us will present."

Joey shrugged and Clarke smiled, they had agreement.

✳   ✳   ✳

The fire was roaring. The food had been good, and the wine was even better. Being well fed and properly wined took the edge off the anxieties of being on the prowl and being hunted at the same time. Normal Turkish tourists would have skipped the planned strategy session, but these were not normal men. Action was imperative.

Michael spoiled the buzz. "Okay, Joey, let's have it. How and when do you send AA to his heavenly reward?"

Clarke couldn't resist interjecting, "Heaven? You've got to be kidding. Do you think God would let that scum inside the pearly gates? God doesn't like him, and I'm not sure that Alvarez could exist in heaven. He can hardly stand an hour in church; why would he like an eternity with God?"

Joey agreed. "Hell seems like a better place for him. That would be God's best for people that don't like Him. But getting back to the point, I think we would need to wire all three and then see which one he gets into and send that one up."

Michael was curious. "How would we know when that was going to happen? Wouldn't we need to be there all the time to watch?"

Joey nodded. "Yep, we really don't have any other assets. It would be straight surveillance. Who do we trust? In this culture, everyone is on the take. Their loyalty is to the last person that bribed them or the highest bidder."

Clarke looked around and concluded it was his turn. "My take is to enter the hotel as a delivery guy or service person. Once inside, get to his suite and wait for him to return for the night and then do it there with his live-in princess watching, quick and quiet, but not easy. He looks like he can handle himself for a fifty-year-old. He's had a wealth of experience in physical combat, but normally of course he has two big armed thugs holding his victim as he punches."

Michael laughed. "I'm sure he hasn't dirtied his hands in quite a while. His weekly manicures are a sure sign. His hands are so dainty, tattoos and buffed fingernails.

"I see a bit more control in this approach. At least we know he'll go to bed and where he'll be, so we can plan. But how to get in there, that's the challenge. Tell me, what kind of approach would you take to get in unnoticed?"

Clarke didn't seem too concerned. "It doesn't matter. I think a proper tux that looks like I belong at the evening's party. He is known for these lusty soirées, it's a family trait. Naked women popping out of cakes, lines of cocaine on glass coffee tables, more naked women wearing Mardi Gras type masks that encourage threesomes, foursomes, and so on. —On my public golf course at home, fivesomes are welcome on weekends. But absolutely no dwarfs, that is where AA draws the line." Joey and Michael were giggling, partly from a little too much wine, but mostly from a little too much Clarke.

Michael resumed his businesslike demeanor. "Taking a shot is no less risky except that there is a chance I could get away. Tommy, in your scenario I don't see you getting in and out of there with over fifty security personnel. Yes, it would be quick, no shots, but it all would have to go perfectly. If I took a shot from a good vantage point, both of you could be ready to go or already gone, and I could easily join you."

"I'm curious," Joey said. "The only good line of fire I saw was onto the patio restaurant from an elevated position—the top of Hagia Sophia. I don't think they let people up there, especially at night when it's all lit up."

Michael nodded. "I know that, Joey. It would need to be somewhere elevated near there or close enough that I could be down lower. The patio is elevated on the second level, but the slope of the ground up to the church is pretty sharply uphill." He began to draw on his notepad.

Ninety minutes later, they had agreed to do all three with a simple escape plan. Plan A was Michael taking the shot; the fallback was Clarke in the room; finally, if neither of those worked, on the last night there, Joey would ignite the cars when Alvarez left the hotel for the airport. They had only one more day to prepare.

— 24 —

Alonzo Alvarez was careful and curious. He had increased his security force and demanded that his local network comb the region for any signs of his would-be assassin. So far nothing had been found; this gave him momentary relief followed by a constant unsettled feeling.

He had been counseled not to go out during the conference and not to use the same cars for travel but to employ them as decoys; they might draw his enemies. He even had restrictions put on his girlfriend: she was not permitted to leave the hotel, which meant she would spend thousands on hotel services such as private use of the spa.

Alvarez loved clothes, particularly from a tailor in Istanbul with a strange name for an Istanbul resident, Michael Jones. Jones was a British subject who had married a beautiful Muslim woman. He had come to Turkey on holiday and never left, except to do the necessary paperwork to become a permanent citizen. He had lost several hands of poker to AA on previous visits and agreed to make Alvarez a few suits in payment of his gambling debts.

He also provided another service to AA that was their little secret. Alvarez liked young boys, but just as a way to indulge his perverted sense of entitlement. It seemed to be true of men like Alvarez that privilege would allow a powerful person to seek perverted pleasure when normal pleasure was no longer enough.

He considered himself a good Christian who had to get his hands dirty in order to help his people and the truly needy of the world. His charitable foundation gave millions annually to provide fresh water wells in Uganda, spread AIDS education in sub-Saharan Africa, and feed the hungry in the slums of Mexico City. Like many, he lived a duplicitous life where the means to an end were disconnected from his goals. It didn't occur to him that God might be interested in the way he did good as well as the good he did. The fact that he sought to engage in such morally prohibited conduct, in a moderate Muslim country that could destroy his ability to do business there, spoke to his brazen sense of superiority. Even those who favored homosexual conduct did not condone the rape of boys.

It should be no shock to anyone that a man who would sever the heads of his enemies would not have learned to resist his urges. He would not sneak out of the hotel except for one thing, to indulge his tailor's favor. Alvarez was not stupid; he was foolish. As the proverb says, "As a dog returns to its vomit, so a fool repeats his folly."

The evening began predictably for Alvarez and his Carmen. She had ordered seven dresses that afternoon and had chosen the tightest and most uncomfortable one which, of course, was the most expensive, retailing for $4200 US. It was by a new Turkish designer, Ali Barak, who claimed it made a positive statement about the rise of secular Turkish culture. She also knew that no other woman would have the same dress.

AA's reaction was "Holy shit, how did you get into that? Hell, all of your important parts are spilling out!"

She paraded back and forth in front of him. "I'm glad you like it. Later on I will show you how easily it comes off." AA was not known for his ability to emote positive vibes; he simply smiled. She knew he liked it.

AA slipped on his dinner jacket. Then he took Carmen's hand, and they rode the elevator down to the main ballroom for the summit's first official event, a cocktail party. As they exited the elevator bank surrounded by two hulking security guards, they saw but didn't notice the electrical worker.

Clarke had done a great job of disguising himself; he

was most proud of the uniform and tool belt. The ragged Cincinnati Reds baseball hat was a nice touch. He was unsure how he was going to get up to Alvarez's private suite. He was still surveilling the site when his mark came by; luck would be a major player.

Carmen looked Clarke's way, and he did a very Clarkeian thing: he winked at her. Carmen smiled as though it was their little secret. She passed by and then winked back. Clarke hadn't lost his touch; Still got it, he thought.

Now he was even more motivated to get into their suite. Clarke was a man of excessive appetites. No river was too wide, no mountain too high, no wind too strong to assuage the power of his ego.

Alvarez's entry into the ballroom was presidential. He and Carmen didn't descend a staircase, but the doors swung open. They were preceded by tuxedo-clad security guards and accompanied by a string quartet. Nearly everyone looked at Carmen, especially the men, who wondered if her most propitious parts would spill over for their viewing pleasure. The more important eyes, however, were reserved for Alonzo Alvarez's facial expression. Was he in a good mood? Would he be festive tonight, or would he go dark? They needed to know in order to stay in his favor.

The group made their way to the start for the evening, a festive array of gourmet appetizers. AA took a champagne glass and lifted it high: "A toast for my brothers, Carlos, Franco, and Jesús. May they rest in peace only when their deaths are avenged." Tears welled up in his eyes.

The mostly European crowd of fifty answered with cries of "Amen, amen," not surprising from a group of former peasants and thieves who had been raised in the churches, temples, and mosques of Central and Eastern Europe.

It would be an evening of celebration, dancing, and much good food and wine. Alvarez would move from table to table, greeting his flock. But he was not the good shepherd; he was the most feared man in the fashion and gambling world. If you met his expectations and fulfilled your quotas, you were rewarded beyond your wildest dreams. If you performed poorly, you were disposable. If you betrayed Alonzo Alvarez, you were gone, gone from this world.

✻   ✻   ✻

Michael couldn't see much yet from the top of the building he had found a hundred yards away from the restaurant patio and the tables just inside the doors where the Alonzo party now sat in order to eat the evening meal. It had taken him more than an hour to break into an office and get to the top of the building undetected. He had assembled his Guerrilla sniper rifle. It was small and accurate, but only for an expert marksman like Michael was it useful. He was able to put it in his backpack disassembled. It was the perfect tool for a shot of less than two hundred yards. The question would be whether he could get a clean shot. So far Alvarez had not exposed himself close enough to a window in a stationary position for a shot.

He had already been in position for thirty minutes, the wind around ten miles an hour. Not only was it getting cold, but his hands were getting numb and his mind was wandering. It occurred to him that he was no longer the twenty-five-year-old Captain Michael Hart on a mission for his country. The rifle in his hands was not Navy issue, the shoes on his feet were by Nike, the jacket was Hugo Boss, and the pants were REI. What lay on the roof was the body of a pastor, a man of grace and peace, who was about to kill another human being. What would he tell his son one day when asked, "Dad, did you kill anyone in the war?" or "What did you have to do to get those bad men out of our lives?" How was this going to affect his walk with God, his prayer life, his preaching? Could he carry the burden of these acts?

Just then, Alvarez stepped onto the patio for a smoke. What a gift to Michael, the red end of the lit cigarette made it so easy. Michael looked through the scope, he laid his finger on the trigger—and he couldn't pull it. He froze. Alvarez flicked the butt away and stepped back into the room.

Michael rolled over on his back and burst into tears. "I can't do it. What am I doing? Oh God, help me." He seemed numb. He had to go, so he texted Clarke and Joey, "No shot, continue alternative plans." Michael broke down the rifle, slung the bag over his shoulder, descended to the street, and went back to the staging area, a local warehouse that Larsen had arranged.

Joey had not been able to get close to the cars. A guard was posted, and the cameras were on. Clarke, the electrician, was at work on disconnecting them inside the hotel, but first he would need to find where AA's men had put the feed. He had noticed several of the security force in the hotel coming in and out of the same door on the first floor. He figured this could be a staging area or break room or even just a toilet.

Clarke ambled down the hall carrying electrical cord and making plenty of noise with his tool belt. He could now hear voices. He edged up to the room and looked in the narrow slit of a window. He saw three men: one in a suit, very well built, who looked Hispanic, and two other men in coveralls. He surmised it to be one man on AA's detail watching the video feed and two hotel employees on break.

Clarke burst into the room with a big smile on his face. He actually spoke only one phrase, something he thought he could say without revealing he was from Indiana: "*Kaffe orta?*" The men smiled and pointed to the ordinary coffee maker on the cabinet. Clarke smiled, and the coveralls went back to their chess game.

The video man spun around in his chair and asked Clarke a question, a question he couldn't understand. He delayed his answer, pretending to have a mouth full of kaffe orta, and he had grabbed a pastry and took a bite. He stepped toward his questioner and scored a direct hit to his Adam's apple with his thumb. The man grabbed his throat with both hands and collapsed on the floor.

Clarke motioned to the two chess players the international sign for choking. They scrambled to help; he took his victim and positioned himself behind him to simulate the Heimlich maneuver. The two men watched in horror as Clarke jammed his fist into the man's midsection.

He dropped the man on the ground and drew his revolver in the same motion. The horrified men became the confused men as Clarke motioned them toward the utility closet. He tied up the men, gagged and blindfolded them, and left them there.

The video man was dead, not able to breathe with a crushed throat. Clarke dumped him in the electrical closet and disconnected the video feed. He took out his phone and texted Joey, "Video out, go to it." With that, Clarke left the room, ready to find a way to the Alvarez suite.

✳   ✳   ✳

Joey left his position in a nearby café, taking his backpack with three crude homemade-type devices designed to do maximum damage. The only bits of expertise Joey revealed in his preparation of the bombs were his use of Semtex and a couple of wiring tricks. He knew how much to use to get the SUVs airborne.

Joey walked directly to the cars and slid underneath to

the middle section where he attached the magnetic plate on each of the three undercarriages. He would activate them from a phone. He was only in the garage three minutes. As he turned left on the street outside, he texted Michael and Clarke, "All set." He walked up the cobblestone road past the front of the Four Seasons that would take him to the bus that would drop him near the safe house where Michael had already arrived.

As Ludwig reached the front of the Four Seasons, two hulking security types came running from the hotel headed toward the garage. They saw Joey but ran past him full speed. What Joey couldn't know was that the two chess players in coveralls and the dead video man had been discovered. It didn't take long for Alvarez's security force to figure out there was danger in the garage.

✳ ✳ ✳

Clarke was blown; his time was limited. He suspected it might happen that way, but not so quickly. He just didn't want to kill those two chess players.

He had dumped his electrical garb; it was now a liability. Even the Reds hat was down a laundry chute. He now looked more like a rich patron who could afford to stay in the Four Seasons. Under the coveralls was a tuxedo. His Prada loafers had been in his knapsack; the sunglasses, worn at night for effect, topped off his new look. He strolled through the lobby and onto the elevator and punched in the top floor, the same floor on which Alonzo Alvarez and Carmen were staying.

He stepped off the elevator only to find a couple of security personnel; they were looking for an electrician, not an urbane hotel guest. They checked his room key and let him pass. It had been a clever move on his part to take a pass card that would fit every room and closet from one of the chess players.

Clarke slipped into Carmen's personal room attached to Alvarez's master suite. The room was used primarily as storage for Carmen's clothes and fashion samples from the many designers who came bearing gifts for her in order to ingratiate Alvarez. It was difficult to see much by the moonlight, which was the only illumination apart from the various electronic displays that located the television, alarm clock, and glowing light switches. Clarke felt his way to a chair, threw off a couple of boxes, and sat down to wait.

It was moments like this that were the hardest on Clarke—silence, solitude, darkness, and time. There were no distractions. He was forced to be alone with his own thoughts, his own soul. The nagging question always came tumbling in at this kind of moment: "How come I screwed up my life?"

He remembered one of the first verses of Scripture he had asked Michael to memorize: "For we are his workmanship, created in Christ Jesus for good works, which God prepared beforehand, that we should walk in them."

God had prepared a life for him. He was on the path, but bad company, bad habits, and bad events had ruined it all. He felt bound to his dark side, remembering those days when he and his wife Mary were happy together. She was affirming; he was cynical but funny. He couldn't stop trying to control her, criticizing her every move. He would make fun of her choices, her interest in knitting and flowers, and her love of old black-and-white movies. He couldn't seem to stop himself from going dark. It was like a form of self-sabotage.

What was gibbering down deep in his spirit that made him disrespect himself, not to believe he was worth being successful? He had taught Michael that God had accepted him, that God believed in him, and that he had nothing to prove to God. Michael had believed it, and his life showed how redemption really should work. But somehow, Tom never had, and he didn't know why.

He heard the door lock click in the suite, then he heard someone walking fast, and then it went silent. A couple of minutes later he heard a toilet flush and a woman's voice singing, the way people sing to themselves.

Carmen was back, alone. The television came on, and it sounded like she was in for the night. Clarke cracked the door between the rooms. He could see that Carmen was in the bedroom across the suite from the entryway and living room. She had taken off the too-tight evening gown and had not quite decided what to put on, her more important parts were now easier to access for Clarke's well-trained eye. It seemed that she was still young enough that her 38Ds were not also 38 longs. There was something about a beautiful woman half dressed that held a man's interest.

She disappeared behind the door, and this gave Clarke his chance to move into the suite. She emerged into the living room in her nightgown. She was ready for bed, but also for AA or anyone else who might pop in to check on her.

Clarke had a crazy idea: *How about I just step out in the open and we can dance like Fred Astaire and Ginger Rogers?* He usually thought this way after a couple of drinks. But he still had three weaknesses: gambling, drink, and women. There she was in front of him, the unholy trinity; he could have it all. But he thought better of it. Having AA pop in when he was popping Carmen might not be the best idea. He stayed put.

＊　＊　＊

Alvarez now knew about the events of the evening: his dead security man, the disconnected video, the removal of the bombs from the limos, and the missing electrician possibly still wandering somewhere in the hotel. But all this did not stop him from sneaking out with his tailor; he could handle himself. In fact there was something in him that relished a confrontation with his would-be assassins.

* * *

Clarke didn't know that he was the only one left with a crack at Alvarez. Michael and Joey were now back at the safe house, counting on Clarke to use his instincts. Of course that strategy could be disastrous and sometimes was. Clarke nestled up next to and then ducked behind the wet bar.

After over an hour, Carmen summoned a security guard. "Where is AA? Find out when he is coming up!" Her voice revealed her hurt feelings; she didn't like to be cast aside.

A few minutes later, the guard returned. "Carmen, he has left the building with a full security team and didn't say when he would return."

Carmen tried to hide her sadness, but her countenance had fallen. "I'm going to bed; you can lock everything down. Good night." With that, the guard turned off the entry lights and left the suite. The door slammed and the latch clicked shut. Carmen slammed her glass onto the bar, flipped off the light, and went to the bedroom, closing the door behind her.

Clarke was lying alone on the floor behind the bar. Now what? He started laughing silently. He was considering slipping into the bedroom and sliding in next to her, but that could go very wrong. But wouldn't a frustrated lady who knew her man was out enjoying a boy be more open to taking her own pleasure? Still, it didn't accomplish the mission, and he could lose more than his pride if she didn't respond the way he hoped.

Clarke quietly scooted from behind the bar and slipped back to the auxiliary room that he had come from. He checked the hallway and then reentered it and headed down the interior stairs. He was hoping Alvarez's men hadn't stationed anyone on the stairs. They would be fools not to, but knowing many fools, Clarke took the stairs as a calculated risk.

He had only one more floor to go when he saw a head pop up from below. Then he heard the crack of a walkie-talkie, Clarke lunged through the second floor exit, finding himself on the mezzanine level. He walked briskly past the darkened shops and was headed for the EXIT TO STREET sign when he heard, "Halt. Stop, or I will shoot," in pretty good English.

He looked back and saw a lone security guard with a handgun trained on him. He stopped and turned to address the guard. "Hey, my friend, why are you pointing that at me?" Clarke put on his best James Bond devil-may-care demeanor. Two more security guards joined them, pushed Clarke up against the wall, and checked him for weapons.

The out-of-breath older one seemed to have some authority and put the first question. "What are you doing walking the stairs, and why are you trying to sneak out of the hotel?"

Clarke gave them his incredulous look. "Hey, gentlemen, I'm a tourist. Frankly, I've been seeing a hotel guest without her husband's knowledge. I wanted to make a quiet exit." Clarke gave them a bit of a smile.

His captors were in no mood. "We've had one of our men killed here tonight. We are going to need to get more information before we can release you." With that, they pointed to the elevator. Clarke was sure he couldn't get on it; torture was not part of his plan.

Just as the elevator door opened, he intentionally tripped himself, causing two of the three guards to stumble. This gave him just enough room to grab a guard's arm and take his gun. He pushed the guard away and pulled the other one across his body as a shield. Clarke fired once, and the bullet hit the older guard's forehead front and center. He turned and did the same to the one still on the ground next to him. The third guard had his hands in the air; he wanted no part of what was coming.

Clarke turned him and barked, "Get me out of here. Show me the way out."

The guard was eager to help. "Okay, please, just don't kill me. It's this way, out that door," he said, pointing to an exit. They went out the door onto the wet cobblestones from a surprise cloudburst. They were now fifty yards down the street. Clarke ducked into an alley and slammed the guard's head against the wall. The man slid down it to the ground, unconscious. Clarke walked on till he found an all-night taxi stand. He gave the safe house address to the driver.

He had enough sense to direct the taxi driver to a false address half a mile from the real destination. When he finally arrived, he made enough noise to wake Michael. Joey was already behind the door with his gun drawn in case Clarke had led his captors to them under duress. Clarke, as usual, was first to talk,

"Crap, O for three tonight. I almost didn't make it, boys. I killed three men just to get here and left another one with a major headache. I left Carmen in bed, and Alvarez left her there too. Apparently he went out to see his boys instead of servicing Carmen."

Michael sighed. "He is not going to stay around now; he'll be on full alert. Jack says he has more meetings in London."

Joey seemed resigned to their next move. "So how do

we get to London? It looks like another hurry-up-and-wait drill."

Michael nodded. "Yeah, he has at least another day of meetings here with his fashion people, then it's London. We'll go get a place to stay, and then we'll find out where he will be and for how long."

✳ ✳ ✳

It had been two weeks since Jen, Corey, and Janie had arrived at Jack Larsen's ranch. Jen was hoping that it would all end soon and kept looking to Jack for clues about how it was going. There had been no communication with Michael in more than a week. She was beginning to doubt not that he would return safely but that he would be able to return to being his normal self. She wanted to talk to him again; she had told Jack, "Next time he calls for intel, I want to speak with him."

When Jack came down from his office with a satellite phone in hand, he was doing what Jen wanted. "Here, it's Michael for you." She snatched the phone and disappeared into her bedroom.

"Michael! I miss you so much. Are you okay? When will you be home?"

Michael felt emotion churning down deep. "Hi, baby. We are nearly done. I'd say another week and we will be walking hand in hand on Jack's ranch or wherever you want."

She wanted more reassurance. "Will you be okay after all this? Will we all be the same?"

Michael calmed himself. "We won't be the same, but we will be together, in love and moving forward, so I want you to pray for me. Pray that we are successful and that justice is done." He couldn't let his guard down, or he would lose it right there on the phone, and then Jen would fall apart.

"Honey, you hug the kids for me, and just know I love you and I will see you soon. Give me back to Jack."

Jen was still nervous but satisfied that she had heard his voice and he seemed to be in control. She said, "Okay, I love you," and handed the phone back to Jack.

"Jack." Michael was in the summing up mood. "Did you say your intel bunch have AA in London in two, three days?"

Jack was matter-of-fact. "Yeah, and my guys are rarely wrong. They wouldn't have got caught with their thumbs up their ass like our intelligence boys did when the Japanese attacked Pearl Harbor. I have guys in airports, hotels, boardrooms, and situation rooms around the world. They know their stuff." He liked to brag about his intelligence gathering services. "I know you don't like the idea, but you guys check into the Hotel Ibis across from Euston Station. It's cheap and has a good breakfast, and no one will notice you."

At 4:00 AM, the trio boarded a military flight from a private terminal at Atatürk Airport that landed four hours later at Luton Airport, just north of London.

It was no secret that Alvarez would stay at the Savoy. He wanted to be part of the history that was the Savoy, to have breakfast in their famous grill like Lord Olivier and Marilyn Monroe, like Bogart and Bacall. He and Carmen were not speaking after his infamous night out with the boys, but the luxury of the Savoy would assuage Carmen's sudden rush of morality. For all his power, he seemed to be inept with Carmen, even at her mercy. She held sway over him, the Virgin Mary in a tight dress. They didn't understand it; they just lived in its reality.

Life at the Ibis didn't include the accoutrements of the Savoy—the birdcage tea rooms, big-screen TVs, and little bells next to your bed to summon servants rushing to your side 24/7. It had rooms whose size and accommodation said, "Get the hell out of here and see London." This seemed to make sense because Jack predicted two days until Alvarez arrived.

This time, however, there would be no getting into AA's hotel. After Istanbul, with bodies and bombs galore, security would be intense. The strategy would require not only stealth but creativity. It would be back to basics. No long shots or sneaking into bedrooms or planting explosives. This would be close, personal, and direct.

Michael walked past the British Museum with Clarke and Joey as they wandered through the University of London on their way to Soho for a bit of lunch. As they passed a Baptist church, Clarke asked Michael, "Do you miss it yet?"

Michael seemed nonplussed. "Haven't been thinking congregation lately. I'm focused on getting this done and getting away."

Clarke started to muse, "That is a luxury for us, isn't it? Getting away, back to our normal lives? Except I don't have one to go back to. Mine is so screwed, it doesn't draw me. This is better."

Michael shook his head. "Tommy, you know what to do about that. You've created bad habits, and they became your character. Now you throw yourself on God and ask Him for the help you need to reverse your field. You can learn good habits again, which will reform your character. You can get it back."

Clarke rolled his eyes. "Oh, you mean after I've finished killing a few more people, I can get my good vibe with God again?"

Michael stopped walking and faced Clarke. "Being a cynic is not the answer. You know why this is happening. If there were another way that protected my family and preserved my life, I would take it. This is a moral dilemma. There is no good choice, and we have taken the least evil bad choice. We can return good for evil, we can love our enemies, but God himself cannot end all evil without resorting to violence. He can't love Satan to repentance and reconciliation. If he could have, he would have. So God has to do Armageddon to destroy evil. That is what we're doing, get it?"

Michael turned and started walking again. Joey trailed, just listening. Clarke said, "Okay, I've got it, Reverend Hart."

Normally Michael's London itinerary would include a couple of hours in the British Museum looking at Assyrian artifacts and Near Eastern history. Now that the important biblical manuscripts were at the British Library on Euston Road, he decided to pass by. Clarke and Joey's only interest in the museum was the restored circular reading room where Karl Marx used to hang out and wrote *Das Kapital*. But hunger overruled, and they headed for a nice little restaurant in Soho.

"I like the lunch here; pretty good for ten quid." Clarke liked to use British slang, it made him feel native.

Joey squinted as he looked up at the sun. "Can you believe it? The sun is out only 62 percent of the time now, and this is the sunny season. I wish I were back with Cheryl in Naples."

Clarke laughed. "Were you thinking Naples or nipples? Cheryl always reminds me more of the second."

Joey laughed. "Both, I suppose."

Michael enjoyed the banter but wanted to get serious. "Do you guys agree with me that this time let's use the more direct approach, close and personal?" Both nodded because their mouths were full of bread and soup.

"The premium is to get it done and get away, and get home." Michael was emphatic.

"The challenge is where and when, how, et cetera." Joey seemed more intense in his opinion.

Clarke pointed a finger. "I want us to really think this through. It should be simple and direct, so simple that they would never expect it."

Michael sat back and said, "I'm listening."

Joey was excited. For the first time, he seemed to have a brainchild. "Disguise—we need to find a way to get one of us close to him and then strike. I don't think it will work for all three of us to be close or even two, but one of us, that's doable."

Rather than retire back to the Ibis, where the rooms were too small for three, they decided to talk it through en route as they strolled through Covent Garden, a charming shopping area with open-air cafés, street entertainers, stylish shops, and markets. To focused men like Michael, Clarke, and Joey, it was an outdoor mall, like Hong Kong without the heat and humidity.

Michael wanted to visit a former pub, now a coffee-house, named Boswell's, where Dr. Johnson first met his good friend and biographer. Johnson had been dead over three hundred years, but for those who had read him, he was unforgettable. Boswell once wrote that when Johnson wrote, he dipped his pen in his own heart. Michael recalled one of his better lines: "Be not too hasty to trust or to admire teachers of morality: they talk like angels, but they live like men."[2]

Johnson was best known for producing the first complete dictionary for the English-speaking people. He was the man who established English as a lingua franca for the world. It took him ten years; he had enough money for three, and it should have taken him less than five. Michael liked Johnson because he was brilliant but greatly flawed. Michael saw himself the same way, as a man of skill, of great learning, but living like a man instead of an angel.

[2] *Yale Works: Rasselas and Other Tales, XVI: 87, 74.*

The coffee shop was a disappointment. It wasn't a pub, and its coffee was normal. Joey rolled his eyes as they walked out. "Wouldn't want to miss that. I'd better put it down as a 'must do' when I bring Cheryl over here."

Clarke smirked, "Yeah, I'm sure that will be quite titillating for Cheryl."

Joey gave Clarke a "that's enough of that" look.

By the time they had walked through Leicester Square and down into Trafalgar, past Lord Nelson and through St. James's Park into Westminster, they had hatched a plan. It was perhaps a crazy plan, but they believed in it. As they passed the Horse Guards grounds, Joey pointed out that it was the site of the 2012 Olympic beach volleyball match where Misty May and Kerri Walsh won their third gold medal for the United States. Most Americans knew more about that than the history of the Queen's Household Cavalry. Misty and Kerri looked better in their outfits than any horseflesh.

Clarke had had enough of Michael's history lesson, and Joey had had enough of Clarke's comments about Cheryl. It was time for them to work on the plan. Joey was first: "I'll see you guys tonight for drinks in the bar, say 6:30. We can check in then."

Michael was always nervous when the three were together; he was even more nervous when they were on their own. "Okay," he said, "remember, we are working, but we need to kill two days. Get your work done before you play."

Clarke nodded agreement, already knowing what he needed to do.

Joey took the Underground to Notting Hill, thinking he might see Hugh Grant and Julia Roberts sunning themselves in the park. He'd heard you could find a lot of secondhand shops there, and that was what he needed. Clarke walked away back toward Trafalgar Square; no one expected he would end up in the National Gallery. Michael turned around and spied Winston Churchill in Parliament Square. His statue was a very good likeness. No one was a bigger fan of Churchill than Michael. It really ticked him off that protestors had urinated on their national hero's statue. He entered Westminster Abbey, where the plaque in the floor said, "Remember Winston Churchill." Many famous men would not have liked such a plaque; Churchill would have relished it: "Yes, do remember me. I saved Western civilization. Twice."

Periodically Michael reminded himself, You're not a tourist. It was painfully obvious that he was on mission, but he was behaving as a tourist. Hiding in plain sight, looking at stuff, was about as safe as it could get. His dark green baseball cap and sunglasses helped some, especially since the sun was out.

He strolled through the abbey, pondering the once great kings and queens buried there. One of the ironies of familial conflict meant that the tomb of Queen Elizabeth I was located in the same space as that of her sister, "Bloody" Mary I. The church was filled with tourists, not exactly what Jesus had in mind when He promised to "build my church." Most people of the last generation remember the abbey as where Queen Elizabeth II was crowned and where Princess Diana's life was celebrated and Elton John sang a song in her honor. Michael's mission was murder, but he planned to spend all day in church.

As much as Westminster Abbey was a part of the English identity, St. Paul's Cathedral was a more practical working church. It was a place where the average guy could wander in on a Sunday morning and attend worship. It was where Charles and Diana were married and where Churchill was memorialized in 1965. St. Paul's boasts the second largest dome in Europe after St. Peter's in Rome. The church has been around in one form or another since in 604. It burned and was rebuilt by Christopher Wren in 1635.

The first stop Michael wanted to make was to the John Donne tomb, where one can see his death mask and remember the pastor/poet who penned, "No man is an island." He sat down for the 11:00 AM service, and the majesty was breathtaking. He looked up at the dome and took in the magnificent storytelling on the dome. There it was, the gospel, the good news, why it is all worth giving your life to. The nave, transepts, and choir were arranged in the shape of a cross. Being a Churchill fan, he recalled that at his funeral, two buglers stood in the dome, one to play "Taps," followed by a second to play "Reveille," symbolizing death and resurrection.

The organ began to play, the sound filled the cathedral with its glory, and the choir processed through the adequate crowd followed by the clergy. The entire service was an oasis from Michael's emotional storm, and he realized this could be his last time in any formal worship with other followers of Christ. It was a moment of transcendence, because all those tourists suddenly were much more: they were worshippers, followers, disciples, children of God.

Michael stepped out of the cathedral and headed down the Strand. He passed the Savoy on his left, which shook him back into his missional mode. It would be twenty-four hours, and then Alonzo Alvarez would be present in that space, eating their food, drinking their wine, enjoying their luxury. Little did he know his days, his hours even were now numbered.

— 25 —

Dinner brought new information. Joey had done some important shopping in Notting Hill and had an outfit he liked. Clarke had enjoyed the tour of the War Cabinet Rooms where Churchill managed World War II from underground, as well as the bar across the street. He was in a very good mood. He was convinced that he could have served with Churchill, but he couldn't have matched him drink for drink. Churchill could put away more liquor than any sober man alive. Clarke had given it a shot. Obviously, judging by his body language and slurred speech, he had failed.

Michael took one look at Clarke and said, "Time off is clearly not good for you, Tommy Boy. We need to get you back to work."

Joey laughed, but he was worried a bit about Clarke's focus when it came down to the kill. He had to comment, "I'm glad we met for drinks." Just then the waitress arrived. Joey pointed at Clarke, "He will have coffee, no sugar or milk."

Michael agreed and added, "I will have a house Merlot. Give my friend"—pointing at Joey—"a Guinness, and only coffee for the drowsy looking fellow."

There were more surveillance cameras in London than taxis, but Michael wasn't worried. They didn't stand out, and no one was looking for them. Officials had no idea where they were. It seemed like the best approach was to walk down Stephenson Way and choose from several Indian restaurants, one that would fill and sober up Clarke so they could have a productive evening. They playfully considered tickets to *Mamma Mia* but felt that Clarke might stand and sing along.

It was midnight before they went to their separate rooms. At dinner, they got word that Alvarez would be arriving the next afternoon and, it appeared, would stick with his plan to stay at the Savoy. That evening, Michael had taken special note of the Victoria Embankment Gardens just behind and below the Savoy. The walks and trails there could provide points of entry and exit if need be.

LONDON TOWN

Alonzo's posse landed at 12:32 PM at London's City Airport. The fleet of cars ferried the group of more than twenty to the Savoy. The fifteen-minute drive was quiet in Alonzo and Carmen's car. She was still mad about his night out with the tailor. Alonzo was not a man accustomed to thinking about pleasing his woman, but in this case his mind was active in how to improve her temper.

He looked at her and asked, "What would you like to do here that you haven't done before? What would be fun for you?" He gave her a big smile.

Carmen cracked a smile, knowing she was in charge. "I've always wanted to ride that big Ferris wheel, you know, the one on the river, the London Eye." She didn't think Alonzo would take her out in public like that, considering his celebrity and the present danger, but she thought it would be a good test for him.

"Whatever you want babe, I will arrange it." Alonzo smiled, patted her on the knee, and asked his assistant to make it happen.

Carmen added one thing: "Oh yeah, make it after dark. It will be beautiful, even romantic. Can we get one of those pods, capsules, whatever they call them, to ourselves?"

Alvarez winked. "I'm sure they will give us an entire car if we pay for it." He was now sure his stay at the Savoy would be better. He had lived the truth of the proverb, "Better to live in the corner of an attic than with a nagging woman."

The entourage pulled up in front of the Savoy, and they were greeted by a fleet of hotel personnel led by a dapper man in a top hat. The Savoy's 150 million pound facelift made it shine. It was stunning in its opulence and first rate in its service. There was nothing you couldn't get at the ring of a bell, twenty-four hours a day. Alvarez took a suite, and his party, including guards, took all the surrounding rooms. His meetings were to be held in his London headquarters on the Strand, only a few blocks away.

The staff at the Savoy were accustomed to street people. The older man leaning on his cane cloaked in an old Macintosh raincoat was just another part of the scenery. Joey had done a great job with the disguise. He had a clear view of Alvarez's cars as they left the premises, but this time they didn't park near the hotel. They sped off back to their home base to be used for other customers. Alvarez had outsourced his transportation after the episode in Istanbul.

Joey's plan was to find out where the chauffeurs were located and how he might replace the driver in the car that Alvarez would enter when he left the hotel. It was then up to Clarke and Michael to play off his success or failure to get the car. The wild card: they had no idea when Alvarez would leave the hotel, with whom, and where he would go. The only thing they could control was the car. That was the key; then they had various options.

It was unlikely that Alvarez would leave with his entire entourage during the day. This was because he would only be traveling a few blocks up the Strand to his offices. This trip would be quick; the only thing it had going for it was they had an idea where he was headed, but still only an idea until he actually pulled up in front of his office.

If he went out at night, there would be a larger group, and it would be social. Again, no idea where he might go. There was one way they could know at least the destination: the drivers would know ahead of time.

This was why Michael and Clarke followed the fleet of cars as they left the hotel. They pulled into a car park two miles away near the Barbican Business Park. BARCLAY CAR SERVICE was the insignia on the door. It was clear they were using ordinary working drivers and not any professional security to drive the cars. Michael noticed the drivers milling around the office.

Michael's wheels were turning. "Looks like they are just hanging out. Either they are on call or have more appointments. We need to see their schedule."

Clarke already had an idea. "What if I go ask to rent their car for a while and ask them when they have openings? That would tell us at least when they are booked."

Michael was impressed. "Good one, Tommy Boy, that will help." Clarke walked up to the driver's room and stepped in. The smell of incense filled the air; it reminded him of a few places he had been. He picked out the Anglo behind the desk,

"Hey, bud, how does a guy rent a car around here?" Clarke's manner made it easy to enter a room. Hardly anyone moved, only two of five looked up.

"American, eh?" The scheduler flipped open his book. "What are you looking for, what kind of car, and when?"

Clarke said, "Tonight about 8:00 PM, a stretch for about seven passengers."

The scheduler ran his hand down the page. "Sorry, mate, all our cars are booked. Big party at the Savoy. We can go earlier or later."

Clarke thought this was too good to be true. "What time would later be?" He held his breath.

"It's only booked for ninety minutes, to go to the London Eye—you know, the big Ferris wheel. Then straight back to the hotel."

Clarke showed appropriate disappointment. "Ugh," he said with a sigh. "Think I'll need to go elsewhere; thanks anyway." He walked calmly back to the car, thinking, *We have something to work with here.*

He hopped back in with Michael. "It sounds like a party needing three SUVs will be leaving the Savoy at 8:00 PM for the London Eye. Do you think Alvarez would ride the Eye?"

Michael shrugged. "I don't have a clue, but someone in the hotel intends to. We could plan around it; we have nearly seven hours to prepare." Michael turned the car around and headed back to pick up Joey.

Joey had gone up the Strand and moved onto a side street. He had stepped into a pub, changed his clothes in the men's room, sat down at the bar, and ordered a beer. He then walked to the agreed-on pickup site in front of the National Portrait Gallery until he saw Clarke waving at him. He jumped into the car. Ten minutes later they returned the car to the hourly rental and took the Underground to the Embankment so they could have some lunch and discuss the possibilities before them.

They walked along the footbridge over the Thames nearest the London Eye, wondering what might be done. Michael was skeptical: "We don't know if the party going there is Alvarez, and if it is, how we might take advantage." He lifted his sunglasses as he squinted into the milky sky at the Ferris wheel turning ever so slowly. He added, "If we can confirm that it's them, then we can make a plan."

Joey laughed. "The only way we can confirm is if they walk out of the hotel and get into the cars."

Michael frowned. "That's not good enough, Joey. You wouldn't have time to replace the driver!"

Joey had a moment of rare brilliance. "Michael, if they get into the car, we don't need to change drivers. We know where they're going; the key is what happens after they get out of the car. We concentrate all our energy on that moment. If they're the wrong party, then we live to fight another day."

Michael smiled. "Yeah, you're right." He paused. "All right, what do we know?"

Clarke was reading off his phone: "The London Eye takes forty minutes to rotate once. Each capsule holds from three to twenty-five people. You can get VIP treatment for extra price and red carpet valet service so you don't have to share a capsule. I would propose that is what Alvarez is going to do: get out of the car and be ushered up to the wheel, and then he and his babe are going to have a romantic trip over the city. Why else would he take a chance like this? She must be the one who wants to do this; I'll bet you it's personal, not a business deal. He will have three cars, one for himself and family, one for security, and one for the entourage, the helpless, the hapless, and the hopeless."

Michael nodded, "Nice alliteration; you missed your calling—I'm serious."

Clarke smiled. "Michael, I've missed a lot." It was time to plan. Joey would be at the Savoy to confirm that the Alvarez party was actually coming; then he would provide transportation out of London. Clarke would use his electronic skills, and Michael would do the kill. Their plan was ridiculous, but then these were men who were accustomed to the ridiculous—as in miraculous.

— 26 —

Alonzo Alvarez thought by now he wouldn't have to go through with it, but he had resigned himself to the reality. "The bitch insists on going to that Eye thing." He rarely let on about Carmen to his assistant, but this was really getting to him. He was accustomed to having his way, but she was holding fast: no sex until after she got her turn on the big Ferris wheel. He was thinking he might just get alone with her and have his way on the damn Ferris wheel.

His day had been a full one as several groups came to see him, all representing various clothing lines wanting Alonzo's worldwide network to distribute their latest fashions. Tomorrow he would go to his office and make the final decisions, and then it would be home to New York for an extended stay.

One meeting was not on the printed agenda; none of his business associates knew anything about it. He entered the elevator and went down two floors to a suite with three men. They were in charge of Alvarez's other business, the get even business.

He didn't bother to shake hands, "Okay, what went wrong out there in New Mexico?" He had that bloodless look in his eyes that many a dead person had seen just before the end.

"Mr. Alvarez"—a very sophisticated-looking man cleared his throat and attempted an answer—"our men went into what we thought was a single defender situation. Either he had the capability of two or three men or there were three or four men. Our two men are dead. Do you want us to try again?"

Alvarez seemed puzzled. "I thought he was an old retired guy. Yes, I want you to send as many in there as need-

ed. I want bodies; I want to show this padre some bodies."
With that, Alvarez left the room and went back to looking
at blazers and skirts.

✳   ✳   ✳

Michael was just about prepared. He had all the equipment that was needed; it was all stored in his backpack.
He didn't plan to get through London Eye security with it.
His entrée would be unique. Clarke had his electronic gear,
very simple: two instruments slipped into the pockets of
his REI camping trousers.

They both sat near the big wheel in the park below,
waiting for a text from Joey. That text would tell them they
would go out to a late dinner or they would be carrying
out the most dangerous mission they had in years: no tech
support, no backup helicopters, no cavalry to save them.

Alvarez thought it ridiculous that Carmen demanded
they dress in formal wear for the Ferris wheel. They looked
good, and she insisted on having pictures taken before they
went down to the cars.

Joey sat patiently in the lobby, reading the *London
Times*, waiting to see if Alvarez was indeed the party going
to the Eye. When he first saw Alvarez's security come off
the elevator, he knew it was probably them.

When he saw Alvarez in a tux and Carmen on full dis-
play in a long gown, his heart sank. He thought, *They won't
be going to the London Eye dressed like that.* He got up to
follow them out and saw that the drivers were of the same
description that Clarke had given them, Barclay Car Service. His text to Michael was "Game on." And with that,
he headed to the car that Jack Larsen's men had provided.

Michael positioned himself near the line of people
waiting their turn to ride the wheel. This time of night,

the more romantic types were out. They wanted to propose marriage, impress someone on a first date, or make a toast, something special. London after dark on the famous London Eye was worthy of special effort and even a reservation. Michael strolled past the lines and stood off to the side like many who just wanted to see the Eye but not ride it.

Clarke eased up to the control building, where the electronics of the wheel were managed. He wasn't sure what he would find, but he was sure he could break it. He knew that each capsule had a surveillance camera and sound capability, and he was sure escape hatches of some kind were located on each capsule for emergency purposes. Once Alvarez was on the wheel, it would take forty minutes for the capsule to rotate back around, and whatever capsule he was in would need to have all sight and sound turned off.

It only took the Alvarez party nine minutes to pull up in front of the VIP slips for cars. Security jumped from the lead car and surrounded the vehicle from which Alonzo and Carmen emerged. Hand in hand, they strolled toward the Eye. The Eye never actually stops; the timing was important so that Alvarez and Carmen would not have to wait when they reached their special capsule. Michael's timing was even more crucial: he had to surmise which was their capsule and sync his move.

Alvarez decided that he and Carmen would violate the at-least-three-people-in-a-capsule rule and take one for themselves. She thought it was romantic; he wanted to be alone with her so he could become the first member of the London Eye Club, for those with the cojones to take their woman on the ultimate ride while over the city. Alvarez's security force knew about it and were instructed to drop back at the last moment.

The capsule came around, moving very slowly. Alvarez and Carmen stepped on. Michael was starting to move and saw the security guards stand back. He was a bit puzzled, but quickly from an angle out of the party's eyesight he jumped the turnstile and was on the capsule with Alonzo and Carmen. Michael's research had paid off: he closed the capsule door before security could react. But they didn't understand what had happened; it looked like some crazy was trying to get a free ride, so they didn't draw their weapons. They were more afraid of Alvarez than worried about him.

They turned immediately and looked for the operator. "Hey, stop the wheel. There's a guy who jumped in with them. He shouldn't be there."

The operators didn't know what to do. The young man helping people into and out of the capsules held up his hands. "We can't stop it. You have to go to the building over there and talk to them." He pointed at the control building which Clarke had taken over; two more people were tied up in a closet. He also had disabled the sight and sound from the capsule that held Alvarez, Carmen, and Michael.

Clarke opened the door and greeted the two security guards. "Hey, boys, how can I help you?"

They seemed unsure of themselves. "Hey, you've got to stop the wheel. There is a guy who jumped on with Mr. Alvarez. We don't know who he is or what he's doing."

Clarke looked up at the capsule which now had moved to twenty feet above the river,

"And do what, boys?" Clarke pointed up. "If I stop it now, there is no way to take them out of there without bringing in special equipment. It takes an act of Parliament to stop the big wheel. I don't hear any screaming, and I don't see it rocking. I think you boys should get a cup of coffee or tea and wait forty minutes and it will be back down. I'm sure Mr. Alvarez will have a story to tell. If anything goes wrong, I will call in special forces, but until that happens, maybe they'll make friends up there." Clarke gave them his winning smile.

"Okay," the older guard said. "We'll wait right here. If anything happens, tell us immediately."

As they walked away, the younger one said, "Boy, AA is going to be pissed."

Pissed was not probably the word that best described Alvarez's thoughts. He was about ready to piss down both hind legs, was more like it. When Michael jumped on the capsule, AA ordered him off, but when Michael closed the door, he pulled a revolver and ordered AA and Carmen to sit down, and they did.

Alvarez had a sixth sense. "Who are you? You wouldn't be the preacher man, would you?"

Michael smiled. "Amen, brother. I hope you are ready to meet your maker tonight."

Alonzo wouldn't budge. "Hey, pretty boy, I just sent an even bigger team out to the ranch in New Mexico. I expect the bodies of your family to be shipped to me in pieces very soon."

A chill went through Michael. "You'll never see them, Alvarez. They can't get here before you die."

Alvarez laughed. "You better hurry, boy. My guards will be coming to get me."

"How? Are they going to fly up? We have half an hour before anyone can help you."

Carmen stopped crying long enough to beg, "Please don't kill us. We won't kill your family, isn't that right, honey?"

Michael thought a minute. "Phone your thugs and call them off, right now. Then call your guards and tell them you're okay; tell them to relax."

Alonzo took the phone and pushed a button. He began to speak, and whoever was at the other end knew his voice. "Tell them to stop the hit on the padre's family. Yeah, now stop it." Then he hit another button. "I'm okay. This guy is crazy, but not dangerous. Stand down."

Michael sat back. "It's very interesting how reasonable you are when your own butt is on the line. I'll tell you what, Alvarez, I'll give you a fighting chance. I know you come from a tough background, and you know how to handle yourself. You have a lot of blood on your hands. I'm going to put my gun away, and you can try and save yourself."

Alvarez smirked. "You have made a mistake. It will be a pleasure to wipe my ass with your dead hand." Michael found the image disturbing. He put the gun into the backpack, and Alvarez lunged toward him. Michael stepped aside, and Alvarez hit his head against the capsule wall.

Michael embedded his shoe on Alonzo's neck. "Okay, I'll let you up, and you can try again."

Alvarez was startled but got up and lunged again, this time grabbing Michael's right knee. Michael jammed the heel of his hand into AA's neck and pinched a nerve with his other hand. Alonzo roared in pain, and Michael walked him across the capsule like a puppet on a string.

Carmen was screaming, "Stop, stop, don't hurt him!" and clawed at Michael's face. Michael kicked her feet out from under her, and she went down hard, dazed. The capsule was rising higher and higher. Michael thought it was about on top and his time was running short.

Alvarez regained his feet and scored a direct hit with his right fist that jarred Michael and sent him sprawling. Alvarez had that bloodthirsty look and his massive hands wrapped around Michael's neck. It would have taken only a few seconds for most of Alvarez's opponents to die from the crushing force.

But Michael was not most men. Alvarez went flying off him, a simple reaction to excruciating pain in his groin. Michael still had Alvarez in his grip; he let go only to punch the wind from his prey. He quickly turned Alvarez around, and broke his neck with one swift jolt. Alvarez dropped onto the capsule floor, dead.

Michael didn't take time to enjoy it. He took rope and tape from his backpack, tied up and gagged Carmen, and laid her gently on the capsule floor. He pulled a glob of Semtex from his pack and pressed it into the corner and set the fuse. He set the timer and began to survey where the capsule was situated.

He took out his phone and sent a text to Clarke and Joey: "60 seconds." Joey started the car engine and began to drive toward Westminster Bridge. Clarke slipped out of the control building and started toward the bridge on foot, a quarter-mile away.

Michael pulled the mini-chute from his pack. It had worked for short jumps before. A few hundred feet is too short for a conventional parachute, too far for newfangled wings or superhero suits. But this little invention of special operators had proven to work 75 percent of the time.

The capsule had now crested the top of the wheel. No one was paying attention except the two worried security guards; they looked up now and then but had noticed nothing unusual. Suddenly they heard a sound and saw a ball of fire come from the capsule. Debris was flung in all directions, there was screaming, and the great London Eye's automatic shutdown mode had been activated. Sirens began to whine, and emergency lights were flashing. Michael was flung out according to plan and lost in the darkness. Everyone's eyes were riveted on the fire and the sight of two bodies falling into the Thames.

He had a harder-than-expected landing on the walkway beside the river, where he tumbled into a patch of grass and hedges. Only a few walkers were out; remarkably, they didn't notice him, thanks to the fire on the Ferris wheel. All eyes were fixed skyward.

He crammed the chute back into his pack and started

walking toward Westminster Bridge. He climbed the stairs to street level and stood patiently. Some others joined him at the walkway waiting for the light to change in order to cross. They were all talking about the explosion. He noticed that Clarke was one of his fellow pedestrians.

They set off when the light changed and kept their eye on the road for Joey. They made it across, and in a few seconds Joey pulled up. They hopped in and were off to Biggin Hill Airport just south of London. Jack Larsen used it for moving his men around the world. It was known for no customs service, which worked very well in this case.

It took three days of small planes and small airports, but finally Michael landed in Taos, New Mexico, and soon would see his family again. Clarke and Joey had returned to Florida; Clarke to Naples, Joey to Nipples.

— 27 —

Jack picked up Michael at the airport. The trip to the ranch was a good time to debrief. Michael had only one missional question: "Do you think we got away with it?"

Larsen shrugged. "You are clean in Europe. Your body count was three in Istanbul and two in London. There is no official evidence that anyone fitting your name or description stayed in any hotels, rented cars, or purchased food or any missional materials, since my guys did most of that for you.

"There are no men left alive in the Alvarez family. The women wanted no more violence that would kill their boys. The security guards don't care; they are out of work. If there's no pay, they no care. The police, Scotland Yard, no one really has a clue. They think Alvarez's past finally caught up with him. As we expected, since your disguises were so simple and very effective, the surveillance videos didn't tell them enough, and since we have erased you guys from all databases, you can't be found because you don't exist. But there is the Atlantic City problem and the Indy problem."

Michael nodded. "Yeah, I'm not sure what'll happen when I return to Indy. I think the police will want to talk to me."

"I agree, but it depends on how curious they are. Sometimes police are very passive when they think justice has been done to cop killers."

Michael smiled. "Hope so."

A few minutes later, they pulled up to the house. Jen, Corey, and Janie ran to greet him, everyone collapsing into each other's arms. It was sweet, and they didn't want it to end.

* * *

The next morning, after breakfast, Jen and Michael were ready to take a long walk. It was time to reconnect about life together. For the first time in nearly a month, Michael was not planning to kill someone.

"Jen, I'm so glad it's over. It was a living hell. I'm just not that guy anymore."

She was curious. "How were you able to do it?"

He stopped and they sat down on a boulder. "It was like another person took me over, who knew what to do—more like an alter ego than a demonic force. My reasons were good; my family, my life were all on the line. I felt it was my only choice."

She shrugged. "Not your only choice. You could have just prayed and trusted God with it completely."

She had to say it; he had to answer it. "I must admit, I thought of Gandhi, even of Bonhoeffer. But I think Bonhoeffer said it best: 'Better to do evil than to be evil.' That was what I kept thinking. I was taking on a great evil by doing a smaller evil. But even at that, some people are so evil they don't respond to love, to goodness, Alvarez was one of those people."

He took her by the shoulders and looked her straight in the eye. "I didn't have enough faith for that. I couldn't take the chance that God would let you and the kids die; I would not let that happen. I wasn't sure what His decision would be, but I was absolute about mine. That was why I did it."

She embraced him tightly, and tears flowed. "Is it over, Michael, really over?" She wanted to hear an immediate and firm yes.

"I'm not sure. There is still the police investigation at home. We should know within a few days of our return."

She laughed, wiping her cheeks. "Okay, Reverend Hart,

do you think saving souls will now bore you?"

He smiled. "It's the kind of boredom I long for."

BACK HOME AGAIN IN INDIANA

Jerry Revis put the note on his calendar, "Talk to Hart." He expected the good reverend to return to work on the fourth of the month. It was time to call, his call went through to Millie.

"Yes, Detective Revis. Reverend Hart is back. Is this urgent police business?" Millie's protective instincts were on high alert.

Revis never made anything sound urgent. "If it were urgent, I wouldn't have waited until he returned from vacation, but it is important, and I do need to speak with him today."

"Okay, Lieutenant, how about 3:30 this afternoon?" Millie was firm.

"That will be fine ma'am. See you then." He hung up and turned to Puke. "We're on today. We can find out what his answers are going to be."

Puke looked incredulous. "He could be responsible for up to nine murders. That's hard for us to cover up or overlook."

Revis laughed. "But look who he allegedly killed: cop killers, thugs, lowlifes, and then the entire Alvarez genetic line. He should be given the Congressional Medal of Honor for service to our country."

Puke stayed serious. "How hard are we going to press him?"

Revis looked up from the morning paper. "We will ask him questions, evaluate his answers, look at the evidence, and make a decision."

Puke nodded. "Fair enough."

* * *

Michael knew it was the moment of truth as he stood to greet Revis and Johnson. He calmly said, "Good to meet you. Sit down. Would you like something to drink?"

"No, thanks, Reverend." Revis took out his notebook. He still wrote it all down, like the cops who trained him. No iPads for him or Puke. "Reverend Hart, what have you been doing the last thirty days on your sabbatical-slash-vacation?" He liked to let suspects hang themselves on their own words.

Michael wasn't used to lying in the pastoral mode. He shifted in his chair. "I have been enjoying my family and taking care of a few personal items that I couldn't get done with the busyness of the church. All the stress that we had with the kidnapping of our son, the attack of those men on my wife, the death of Kenny Bohannon—we just needed to decompress, to be alone for a time."

Revis smiled as he listened, scribbling a few lines. He was ready with the next question. "Those two men who killed Kenny, Carlos and Franco Alvarez—did you know they were poisoned in Atlantic City? Did you know about that?"

Michael looked out the window. "Yes, I read about it. I guess they were related to one of the men our family had trouble with. I honestly can't say that it troubled me very much to hear of their demise."

Revis pressed on. "Did you know that just a week ago their older brother Alonzo, a very wealthy kingpin of the fashion industry with a sordid background, died in an explosion on the London Eye?"

"Yes," Michael said. "It must be a tough time for that family, losing so much in such a short time."

Revis went deeper: "It's like someone wanted them all dead. There are rumors that two men were seen in Istanbul and London that were about the same age and build as you and your friend Tom Clarke. You didn't visit Europe in the last few weeks, Reverend Hart, did you?"

Michael gave a stern look. "No, Detective, I was with my family. Tom Clarke, I understand, was in Naples with some friends."

Revis smiled. "Yes, I know. We talked on the phone with Clarke, and a Joey Ludwig and his wife, Cheryl, vouched for him."

Puke was eager to take it further. "Reverend, you certainly had a motive to harm the Alvarez family. They had threatened your family, and from our research, you might have had the means to do them harm."

Michael smiled. "How could I have the means?"

Puke leaned forward and said, "You were Special Forces; you were one of their best. We know this because they protect only their very best, and they certainly are protecting you."

Michael looked puzzled. "Who would 'they' be, Sergeant?"

Puke was a bit flustered. "The Navy, CIA, SEALS, or whatever your group was called."

Michael laughed. "They don't protect forty-year-old vets; what we did wasn't all that secret." Michael never liked to lie, but somehow he felt justified.

Revis was fighting his own morality, his own sense of justice. He had decided what to ask next. "Okay, Reverend, you don't know how all these people got killed, poisoned, blown up. It sure sounds like Jason Bourne type stuff to hear about some superhero or villain who jumps on the London Eye and then disappears into the darkness during the explosion, almost like a Marvel Comics hero."

"Nope, I wouldn't even know how to do that stuff, let alone do it at my age." Michael was now relaxed. He didn't know what evidence they had, but they were not asking the questions he would. Of course, he usually had a knife to the throat of his interviewee.

Revis stood to leave. Puke was surprised but slowly stood as well. "Reverend Hart, thank you for answering our questions. I think we're finished here, and I don't expect that we'll be back. I think that the killers are out of state. This is a matter for those federal agencies that deal with organized crime. Welcome home and back to a normal life." Revis extended his hand; Puke reluctantly followed suit. They turned and left the office.

Michael stood at the window as they drove away. Could it really be over, really over? He knew it would never be over inside him, for he had to live with the memories of what he had done. More puzzling was to understand where his capacity to murder came from and why it was still intact. His soul was now soiled, his conscience hazy, and the clarity of his voice restrained. It would never be the same, but at least God would let him do it, and both of them would find pleasure in it.

He noticed his old nemesis Frank Ewald walking to his car. He had almost forgotten him during the past month as much as anyone could forget such an irritating person. Michael smiled as he considered using his special skills one last time. "What the hell, one more won't hurt."

ABOUT THE AUTHOR

Bill Hull is the author of over twenty books on everything from anxiety disorders to spiritual power. His work has been rewarded and he is renown for being able to tell a story. To find out more about his work go to billhull.net

www.ingramcontent.com/pod-product-compliance
Lightning Source LLC
Chambersburg PA
CBHW060919250626
47159CB00008B/3076